Enjoy all of these American Girl Mysteries®:

THE SILENT STRANGER   A *Kaya* Mystery

LADY MARGARET'S GHOST   A *Felicity* Mystery

SECRETS IN THE HILLS   A *Josefina* Mystery

THE RUNAWAY FRIEND   A *Kirsten* Mystery

SHADOWS ON SOCIETY HILL   An *Addy* Mystery

THE CRY OF THE LOON   A *Samantha* Mystery

A THIEF IN THE THEATER   A *Kit* Mystery

CLUES IN THE SHADOWS   A *Molly* Mystery

THE TANGLED WEB   A *Julie* Mystery

and many more!

— A *Julie* MYSTERY —

THE
TANGLED WEB

by Kathryn Reiss

★ American Girl®

Published by American Girl Publishing, Inc.
Copyright © 2009 by American Girl, LLC
All rights reserved. No part of this book may be used or
reproduced in any manner whatsoever without written
permission except in the case of brief quotations embodied
in critical articles and reviews.

Questions or comments? Call 1-800-845-0005, visit our
Web site at **americangirl.com**, or write to Customer Service,
American Girl, 8400 Fairway Place, Middleton, WI 53562-0497.

Printed in China
09 10 11 12 13 14 LEO 10 9 8 7 6 5 4 3 2 1

All American Girl marks, American Girl Mysteries®,
Julie™, Julie Albright™, Ivy™, and Ivy Ling™ are trademarks of
American Girl, LLC.

The characters and events portrayed in this book are fictitious. Any similarity
to real persons, living or dead, is coincidental and not intended.

PICTURE CREDITS
The following individuals and organizations have generously
given permission to reprint illustrations contained in "Looking Back":
pp. 150–151—from *Painted Ladies* by Baer, Pomada & Larsen. Used with
permission, Penguin Group; photo by The Record Newspapers (girl with
vegetable baskets); pp. 152–153—from *Painted Ladies* by Baer, Pomada & Larsen.
Used with permission, Penguin Group; © Wally McNamee/Corbis (disability
rights activists); pp. 154–155—Bettmann/Corbis (soldier's homecoming);
Oakland Tribune Collection, Gift of ANG Newspapers, Oakland Museum of
California (Vietnam Babylift); *Diet for a Small Planet* by Frances Moore Lappé.
Used with permission, Ballantine Books; pp. 156–157—Durham Food Co-op
(health-food store mural); from *Fanny at Chez Panisse*, © 1992 by Tango Rose, Inc.,
HarperCollins Publishers, Inc. (Chino Ranch vegetables); Lower Eastside Girls
Club of New York Farmer's Market, www.girlsclub.org.

Illustrations by Jean-Paul Tibbles

Cataloging-in-Publication Data
available from the Library of Congress.

TABLE OF CONTENTS

1
FIGURE IN THE FOG

"It's a mystery how we manage to live here at all!" Julie declared. "This apartment is no bigger than my locker at school." She was kneeling on the floor, trying to fit a stack of Nancy Drew mysteries from her overflowing bedroom shelves into the crowded bookcase under the living room window. The November day outside the window was gray and misty.

"Be glad it's small," called Joyce Albright, Julie's mom, from the kitchen where she was mopping the floor. "Housework here takes only a fraction of the time it used to."

"I just wish we had a bigger place," Julie said wistfully. She liked their apartment well enough. It was close to school and Golden Gate Park and was right upstairs from her mom's shop, Gladrags.

But Julie missed the spacious house her family had lived in together in North Beach, on the other side of San Francisco, before her parents' divorce. She missed having her dad at home with them. And she missed having her best friend, Ivy Ling, right across the street.

She finally managed to cram the books into the shelf on top of a stack of her sister Tracy's *Tennis* magazines. *There!*

"At least there's not a lot of floor space to vacuum," Tracy said in a suspiciously bright and cheerful voice. "Right, Mom? And there's a great view!" She glanced out at the foggy afternoon. "When there *is* a view."

Julie turned to look skeptically at her sister. Sixteen-year-old Tracy was not usually bright *or* cheerful these days unless she wanted something. Julie waited—then rolled her eyes when her sister spoke again: "Of course, we *are* pretty far from the grocery store. But don't worry, Mom, because I can just drive there and do the shopping for you! Hey, why don't I go now and buy some stuff for dinner tonight? Let's have fondue!"

Knew it, Julie thought with an inward smile as she picked up her dust cloth. Tracy was always coming up with reasons to use the car. She'd had her driver's license for eight months already and absolutely loved to drive. But their mom still thought Tracy needed more practice on the steep streets of San Francisco and rarely let her take the car.

"No thanks, honey," Mom replied predictably. "I've got a casserole planned."

Tracy turned on the vacuum cleaner with an irritated flip of the switch, and for a few minutes it was impossible to carry on a conversation while she shoved the machine around the small living area. Finally Tracy shut off the roar of the vacuum. "Well, can I drive to the library, at least?"

In the kitchen doorway, Mrs. Albright shook her head. "Not this afternoon."

"But I have overdue books!"

"It's getting late, it's foggy, and it's supposed to rain. Not great driving conditions. Anyway, I want you to help me with the table decorations so everything will be ready for Thanksgiving. I've got an overstock of Pet Rocks down in the shop, so we're going to turn them into Pet Rock pilgrims and turkeys."

Julie grinned. The silly novelties—just ordinary fist-sized rocks in a box!—would make cute holiday decorations. Leave it to Mom!

But Tracy wasn't amused. "Come on, Mom. I've driven in fog before! Besides, Thanksgiving isn't for another week. And why do we need table decorations, anyway? It's just *us*."

"Actually, we're having company," Mom announced. She propped her mop against the refrigerator and came into the living room. "Hank told me about some men he's been helping at the veterans' rehabilitation center. He said there are a few whose families live far away, who don't have anywhere to go for the holiday—"

Tracy rolled her eyes. "So you had to invite them *here?*"

"I didn't *have* to," replied her mom. "But why not? It will be a pleasure to have Hank with us for the holiday, and an honor to give the veterans

4

a good home-cooked meal."

"Sounds good to me," Julie said. She ignored the dark look her sister gave her. They all liked red-bearded Hank, and hosting soldiers who had returned from service in Vietnam and were still recovering from war injuries was a nice thing to do.

"It's going to be completely depressing having old dudes in wheelchairs crowded in here like sardines," Tracy declared. "Can't I go to Dad's instead?"

"You know very well that your dad has to be away from home this Thanksgiving," Joyce Albright reminded Tracy. "His flight schedule is extra busy this time of year. Anyway, you'll enjoy the vets. They're not old men—some of them aren't all that much older than you."

"I don't care," Tracy groused. "It still sounds depressing."

"I think it sounds fun," said Julie, dusting the top of the bookshelf. "I'll help make the decorations as soon as I finish cleaning up my room."

"You are such a Goody Two-shoes!" hissed

Tracy, and she flounced off to her bedroom.

Julie finished dusting the main room and then retreated to her own small bedroom, still carrying the can of polish and the dust rag. She sat at her desk and picked up the mystery she'd finished earlier that dreary day. Nancy Drew had the perfect life! She got to solve intriguing cases, never had to clean the house, and didn't have a grumpy older sister.

Julie tossed the book onto her bed and stared out the window at the damp street. San Francisco in November was often foggy, but this year seemed gloomier than usual. The misty weather matched her mood.

Outside the window Julie saw a girl in a yellow rain slicker coming down the street, walking two dogs, one leash in each hand. When a gust of wind blew the girl's hood off, Julie recognized her school friend, Joy Jenner. Joy earned money as a dog walker and Julie sometimes walked with her. Julie started to open the window and call hello, then caught herself. It was surprisingly easy to forget that Joy was deaf.

Her friend was so good at reading lips that when they were together, talking wasn't much of a problem. But Joy would not hear a call from the window.

Julie admired the way the dogs walked obediently beside Joy, pausing at the curb with her, wagging their tails when she patted them. Wishing she could have a dog of her own, Julie watched her friend turn the corner.

Julie longed for a dog the way her sister Tracy longed for a car of her own—but she knew the landlord's no-pet rule was firm. A small apartment on a bustling city street wasn't the right place for a dog, anyway.

Julie sighed, and turned her attention to a busy spider that was building a web along the top of her window frame. She knew she was supposed to dust every inch of her room, and that would include the window...but the little spider was working so diligently! It would be a shame to wreck such hard work.

What if she kept the spider for a pet? The landlord could hardly object to *that!* It would be her *secret* pet. "I could call you Harriet, after Harriet the Spy," she told the spider. That was another book Julie liked. And besides, the spider was hairy.

Down in the street a figure appeared in the fog—a woman, struggling to hold on to her umbrella against the wind. It was hard to tell how old she was, but Julie could see that she was tall and thin and was carrying a bulging shopping bag. Her long dark hair was pulled back into a straggly ponytail. She scurried, spider-like, along the deserted sidewalk. As Julie watched, she stopped at the apartment building across the street and started poking into all the metal trash cans on the curb. Then she opened her big shopping bag and stowed something inside.

A thief! thought Julie. Nancy Drew would give chase! But . . . was it really theft when the things had already been thrown away? Julie watched the woman cross the street to the corner outside Gladrags. Shifting her umbrella to her other hand, she tugged at the lid of *their* metal trash can. Julie and her sister had helped Mom put out the shop's trash earlier that very day.

The straggly-haired woman lifted out a small battered table lamp. It had a purple base and a shade painted with bright flowers. Julie had thought it was pretty, but Mom had pointed out that the shade was cracked and the paint was chipping. No one had wanted to buy it, so they had thrown it away. Now the woman turned the lamp this way and that. She looked furtively over her shoulder and then stashed the lamp in her large bag. For a second she stared straight up at the window and looked right at Julie. Julie felt a prickle between her shoulder blades. She watched as the woman bent against the wind and disappeared around the corner.

From the living room came the sound of Julie's mom and sister arguing, their voices rising. Julie stared out at the empty street. The trash thief's desperation seemed to linger in the air.

2
NEW GIRL

Julie arrived at Jack London Elementary the next morning and joined her fifth-grade classmates on the playground. Tracy had been grumpy all through breakfast after Mom had said she could not drive to the high school. Julie was glad to be out in the fresh air with her friends, away from her moody sister.

"Hey, did anyone watch *Lost in Space?*" T. J. asked. They chatted about their weekends, and T. J. made everyone laugh by singing theme songs from *The Brady Bunch* and *Gilligan's Island*. Julie sang along. In the middle of the theme from *Gilligan's Island*, a tall, slender girl with long dark hair and a faded jacket edged up to their group, adding her voice to theirs. Her voice was tuneful, and she slid into perfect harmony with T. J.

Julie was surprised not to know who the girl was; when she had run for student body president, with Joy as her vice president, they had learned almost everyone's names. This girl should be in the school choir! Julie wanted to talk to her, but the bell rang and everyone raced off to line up before she got a chance to meet the stranger.

When the class was seated, Julie's teacher, Mrs. Duncan, walked into the room with the dark-haired girl at her side. "Attention please, everyone!" Mrs. Duncan said briskly. "I'd like to introduce a new girl to our class. Please welcome Carla Warner."

A new girl! Julie had been the new girl at school a year ago, and she remembered exactly how it felt—uncomfortable and a bit lonely. She raised her arm extra high when Mrs. Duncan asked who would show Carla around. As Carla slid into her chair, Julie scribbled a note in the corner of her notebook: *Eat lunch with me?*

She ripped the corner off and folded it small. She wrote C.W. on it and handed it to Joy, who passed it to T. J., who handed it to the dark-haired girl when Mrs. Duncan was writing the math assignment on the blackboard. The new girl unfolded the note, scanned it, and looked questioningly at T. J., who jerked his thumb in Julie's direction. Julie smiled and nodded, and Carla Warner beamed back at her. "Thanks!" she whispered. "I'd love to!" Then she blushed as the teacher whirled around from the board with a frown on her face. Mrs. Duncan was super-strict and piled on extra homework whenever she caught students passing notes. Julie stifled her giggle.

At lunch Julie and Carla walked together to the cafeteria. They sat with T. J. and Joy. T. J. was complaining about how he'd had to babysit his younger sisters most of Saturday and didn't get to play football with his friends, and then on Sunday it had rained. "My whole weekend was a washout," he said morosely.

"Mine too," said Julie. "Nothing but house-cleaning and listening to my crabby sister moan about everything."

Joy chimed in with the big news that her

baby brother had learned to walk. Joy's family had adopted a baby from the Vietnam Babylift. Everyone was excited to hear how well he was doing now. Joy communicated using graceful sign language and also spoke aloud in a voice that had once sounded strange and toneless to Julie. Julie liked the way Carla listened carefully, and the friendly way she smiled at Joy. Joy's deafness made some kids uncomfortable, but it didn't seem to bother Carla one bit.

"What about you?" Joy asked Carla. "How was your weekend?"

The new girl heaved a dramatic sigh. "Busy unpacking boxes from our move. It was soooo much work!"

"Where do you live?"

"Oh—not too far from here. Over by Alamo Square. You know those famous painted ladies?"

"You mean those huge old Victorian houses, the ones painted all different colors?" asked T. J. "You live in one of *those?*"

Julie's dad had driven her past some of the brightly hued historic homes. He'd told her that some of the painted ladies had been written about in books and even put onto postcards.

"We had a million boxes to unpack," Carla told them. "It took all weekend, even with all of us helping. And we're still not done."

"Do you have a big family?" asked Julie.

Carla looked around at all of them and laughed. "Do I ever!"

Did she ever! Julie listened in amazement as Carla told them all about her family: Her oldest brother didn't live at home anymore because he was away in college. She had another older brother in high school, *and* a twin brother, *and* a little sister in kindergarten, *and* a baby sister, too—a year old and learning to walk, just like Joy's brother.

"Wow! That's a lot of kids," marveled Julie, feeling a small twist of envy.

"We're a crowd, all right," Carla agreed cheerfully. "Three girls and three boys—just like the Brady Bunch, except that we have the same parents." Then she told them that her parents were both doctors, but her mom was staying home full time to care for the baby.

"I love babies," said Joy. She rummaged in her lunchbox and pulled out a chocolate cupcake packaged in cellophane. "What's your baby sister's name?"

"Debbie," Carla told her.

T. J. laughed. "Hey—just like the 'Little Debbie' cupcake!" He pointed to the brand name on the cellophane wrapper, and they all laughed.

"Where's your twin brother? Whose class is he in?" asked T. J., looking around the cafeteria. "I want to meet him. He should come eat with us."

"Oh, Tim isn't at this school," Carla explained. "He . . . he goes to a private school."

"Too bad," said T. J. "Well, maybe I can meet him after school. Does he like sports?"

"Tim is great at sports. But he's pretty busy after school."

"But how come *you're* not going to private school?" T. J. asked.

Carla told them that Tim was a pianist. "He's always playing and composing stuff. And he's always winning piano competitions.

So he practices for hours after school every day, and he has to go to a school that has a special music program."

"That's cool," Julie said. "Which school?"

"Well, he just started there today—like I just started here," replied Carla. "I think it's called Maxwell Academy."

"Hey—like the coffee!" Joy pointed out the window to the building across the street, which was plastered with a large billboard for Maxwell House Coffee.

"Um, yeah," said Carla with a grin, and they all laughed again.

This new girl is really nice, thought Julie. It would be fun to visit her big house and get to know her large family. Julie was sure they would become good friends.

3
SPY RADIO

Julie invited Carla home after school. Joy walked with them as far as her street, and then Julie and Carla continued on together. Julie pushed open the door to Gladrags, her mother's little shop on the ground floor beneath their apartment, and the bell above the door jangled. Carla stepped through the curtain of beads at the shop door, her eyes sparkling. "What a cute place!"

"Gladrags is my mom's baby," Julie said, feeling proud of her mom. Running the shop was a lot of work, but a lot of fun, too. It was a treasure trove of trendy miscellany: there were racks of Indian print dresses, knitted ponchos, colorful silk scarves, and hand-tooled leather belts. There were glass cases displaying earrings, necklaces, and bracelets, and baskets of charms and beads for making your own. Shelves around the room held pottery and candles, incense, kites, lamps, and wooden toys. A table in the window was full of hand-painted flowerpots, and macramé plant holders hung from the ceiling.

But today there was no sign of Mrs. Albright. Instead, Hank was working behind the counter. He waved to Julie and Carla. "Hello, lovely ladies. The boss has gone off with Tracy at the wheel and left me in charge. They shouldn't be gone too long—just went to the market to buy provisions for our Thanksgiving feast." He smiled at them. "The fellows I'm bringing with me to the party will just be so glad of a home-cooked meal, I doubt they'll notice whether we're eating roast turkey or plain old hot dogs."

"I think it'll be fun to have the soldiers with us on Thanksgiving," Julie said. Then she introduced Carla. "This is Carla—she's new at school. Carla, this is our friend Hank. He works at the rehab center for injured soldiers."

Carla winced. "That must be so hard," she

murmured, and then quickly turned away to look at some silver bangles displayed on top of the counter. She tried one on her wrist.

"Two for a buck," Hank said. "Pretty, aren't they?"

"Yes!" Carla hesitated, then put the bracelet back. "I'll come back when I've got my money with me."

Julie led the way up the stairs at the back of the shop. "I'll be down here till your mom gets back," Hank called after them. "She said she left you a snack on the table."

Julie and Carla hurried up to the kitchen, where a plate of Oreos waited. They each took three cookies and headed for Julie's room.

Carla was good company. She roamed around, inspecting the bead curtain around Julie's bed, her bulletin board, her posters, her bookshelf, and the framed photo of Julie and her sister sitting on the buckboard of an old-fashioned covered wagon.

"That picture was taken last summer," Julie told Carla, "on the last leg of a cross-country trip to celebrate the Bicentennial. We had loads of fun living like pioneers!"

"Sounds cool," said Carla. She plopped herself cross-legged in the center of Julie's bed, as if she'd been Julie's friend forever, and Julie smiled. "My family has had some great trips together, too," Carla said. She described the amazing vacations she'd taken with her large family: They'd gone to Hawaii, Canada, Mexico, and Italy. Julie couldn't help feeling a twinge of envy; the Bicentennial trip had been wonderful, but her family rarely went traveling, and never all together since the divorce. Her mom had to work so hard running Gladrags, and her dad's busy flight schedule kept him away often.

A little later, Julie and Carla made popcorn, shaking the foil-covered Jiffy-Pop pan over the stove and watching as the foil puffed up like a balloon. They talked about what they liked to read and discovered they both loved mysteries.

"I named my spider Harriet, in honor of Harriet the Spy," said Julie. "She's Harriet the Spy-der!"

"*Ew*—you have a pet spider?"

"Only because I really want a dog, but I can't have one," Julie explained.

"Well . . . my sister is named for Nancy Drew!" Carla told her, giggling. "No, really she was named for our Aunt Nancy. Nancy is my kindergarten sister. She can be a pest sometimes. At least my dog doesn't sneak into my room and play with my stuff."

"What kind of dog do you have?" Julie asked eagerly.

"A border collie," said Carla. "And he's *super* smart." She told Julie about all the tricks her dog could do. He could shake paws and jump over hurdles, roll over and play dead, and even search for hidden objects.

"You have to invite me over to meet him!" cried Julie. "We could hide things for him to find."

"Or I could bring him by when I'm taking him on a walk," offered Carla. "You could walk with us."

"I'd love to!"

The girls took their popcorn back to Julie's

room. Julie got out her tape recorder. "Okay," she said into the microphone, "this is KJC radio. Today we present an interview with—*ta-dah!*—Carla Warner, New Girl in Town."

Carla laughed. "What's KJC stand for?"

"Well, West Coast radio stations always start with K. And the J is for Julie, of course, and the C—"

"—is for Carla!" finished Carla. "That's good. Or we could call it KSPY. Because we both like spies."

"That's even better," said Julie, rewinding the cassette tape. "I'll start over." She spoke dramatically into the microphone. "This is KSPY, best station in the West. And today's interview features the famous Carla Warner, New Spy in Town!"

"You can't tell people I'm a spy," objected Carla. "It's supposed to be *secret*."

"Oh, right. Sorry."

They started again, giggling. Julie asked Carla about her dog. "What's his name? Our listeners would dearly love to know."

"Jack," she said. "Blackjack the border collie."

"How fascinating," said Julie in her radio voice. And can you tell our listeners what it's like to have a twin brother?"

Carla rolled her eyes and made a gagging noise. "No," she corrected herself. "That's unfair to Tom. Usually it's lots of fun having a twin."

"I thought his name was Tim," said Julie.

"Nope—Tom is my twin brother," said Carla, tossing her hair quickly off her shoulders. "Tim is my *older* brother. The one in eleventh grade. Tom can be a lot of fun, but Tim is usually a pain because he's in high school and thinks he's really cool. Todd's okay, though. He's the one in college. College guys are a little more mature than high school guys."

"High school guys?" Tracy popped her head inside Julie's room. "I'm Julie's sister," she told Carla. "Who are you—and what was that about high school guys?"

"This is Carla," Julie said. "Her family just moved here. And her brother Tom is in eleventh grade. I mean *Tim*."

"At the high school? Cool! Maybe I know him."

"No, he goes to Maxwell Academy," Carla replied.

"Hmm. Well, maybe I can come to your house and meet him," said Tracy with a grin.

"Sure—but he's awfully busy," said Carla. "He has practice for football and basketball and stuff. And he plays the piano and practices that, too. So does my twin brother. Tim plays piano, and Tom plays guitar. They want to make a band with our oldest brother, Todd. He plays the saxophone, but he's in college now and doesn't have a lot of time. Maybe they'll make their band in the summer. And when they do, I'm going to be the singer."

"Hey, like the Partridge Family!" Julie pointed out. It was hard to keep the names of Carla's many siblings straight. "But I thought it was Tom who played the piano. Didn't you tell us that at school?"

Carla laughed. "We all play the piano, but some of us play a lot better than others! In fact, everybody tells me I'd better just keep my *voice* as my instrument."

"You *do* have a great voice," Julie said, remembering Carla's singing on the playground with T. J.

"Maybe you'll be like Joni Mitchell or Carly Simon when you grow up," said Tracy.

Carla smiled. "I'd love that," she said. "But my mom says I have so many stories in my head, I should write adventure novels."

"Or mysteries!" suggested Julie.

"Yeah—but I think I'd be a good master spy."

"Me too. Or a detective. My friend Ivy and I want to open a detective agency someday."

"My dad's a—" began Carla, then bit her lip.

"A what?"

"Well, he's a doctor, like I said. But he told me he'd love to be a detective."

"Spies are much more *glamorous*," Tracy said, raising her eyebrows archly. "Like in those James Bond movies." Then she left them, calling "Ta-tah, dahlings!"

The girls curled up on Julie's bed to continue talking about their future plans. Sometimes Julie was sure that being a detective would be the perfect job for her, but other times she wanted to be an ecologist and save endangered species. Sometimes she wanted to become a mayor or a senator—maybe even run for president someday. "Sooner or later," she told Carla, "America will have a woman president. So why shouldn't it be me?"

"It would be cool to live in the White House," Carla said. "Although it feels like our new house is *nearly* that big!"

If only she and Mom and Tracy still lived in a house—just big enough to have a border collie, Julie thought fleetingly. Carla was lucky.

Mrs. Albright came home, and Julie introduced her new friend.

"Would you like to stay for dinner?" Mom asked Carla.

"Oh, please stay!" cried Julie, but Carla shook her head.

"I have to get home," she said. "To help with the baby, and everything."

Tracy popped out of her bedroom and

grabbed her mom's arm. "I'll drive her! Okay, Mom? Can I drive her? *May* I?"

"Hmmm," said Mrs. Albright, considering. She stared up at the ceiling for a moment, then winked at Julie and Carla. "Do you think if we ask Tracy very, *very* politely, she might *possibly* consider driving Carla home?" Her voice was teasing. Tracy gave a yelp of assent and hugged her mother. Then, beaming, she hurried to get the car keys.

"Oh, good," said Julie. "I'm coming too!" She wanted to see Carla's painted lady house.

But Carla was shaking her head. "No, that's okay," she said. "It's not far, really. I really should walk—I need the exercise." She grabbed her book bag and headed across the living room.

"But it's getting dark," objected Mrs. Albright. "And it looks like rain again."

"Really, I'll be fine," Carla insisted.

"Well, come over again soon," begged Julie. "We can play spies! Or else bring your dog and we'll go for a walk—"

"I will," promised Carla. "Thanks for having

me. See you again soon!" She was out the apartment door and down the stairs before Julie could say another word.

Tracy sighed. "Guess *she* doesn't trust my driving either," she said glumly. "Nobody does."

"Now, Tracy dear, you know I trust you," said Mrs. Albright. "You did just fine getting the groceries, and didn't I just give you permission to drive her home?"

"Yes, but—"

"Mom," interrupted Julie, "can't we move into a bigger house so that I can get a border collie? *Please?*"

4
PUZZLE PIECES

At lunch in the school cafeteria the next day, Julie and Joy traded halves of their sandwiches. Julie's mom had packed her a ham and cheese sandwich, while Joy had peanut butter and strawberry jam. They also traded a cookie apiece: Julie had Oreos, while Joy had brought home-baked oatmeal. Julie wished her mom had time to bake cookies. Once she and Ivy had baked Chinese almond cookies together, and they'd turned out pretty well. Maybe next time they would make oatmeal cookies, and Julie would bring some to school. T. J. sat across from them, watching the daily trade, and kept trying to sneak bites of their sandwiches and cookies.

Carla slid onto the bench next to Julie and opened her brown paper sack. She withdrew an apple, a chunk of cheese, and a small green pepper.

"*That's* your lunch?" asked T. J.

Carla frowned at him. "Why not?" She bit into the pepper. "It's a perfectly good lunch. My parents are doctors, and they say fruits and vegetables are healthy and nutritious." She finished the pepper and started crunching the apple.

"You can have one of my cookies," Julie offered.

Carla hesitated, then took the Oreo. "Thanks." She stuffed the cookie into her mouth.

"So much for healthy and nutritious," T. J. teased.

Carla shot him a glare.

"Sorry!" he said. "Want half of this sandwich, too? I'm sick of peanut butter and jelly."

Carla hesitated, then reached for it. "Um . . . okay," she said and wolfed it down.

Julie finished her sandwich. "Lunch will be over in five minutes. Let's go out to the playground before the bell rings."

Outside, the playground was dotted with

kids wearing brightly colored jackets. Julie, Joy, and Carla walked over to the swings, while T. J. chased off after some boys playing kickball. The girls pumped their legs, swinging higher and higher. Julie leaned back and looked up at the tree branches spreading like black fingers across the gray November sky. She felt as if she were flying. How fabulous it would be to soar across the sky like an eagle and perch on one of those black branches . . .

"Hey, Nancy!"

Carla's voice jolted Julie out of her musings. She opened her eyes and saw Carla waving at some little kids who were playing hopscotch on the other side of the playground.

"That's my kindergarten sister, Nancy," Carla told Julie and Joy. "Nan for short."

"In the green hat?" asked Julie.

"Yup." Carla called Nan's name again and waved, but the child was busy with the game and didn't look up.

"Nan is a cute name." Julie wished again that she had a little sister. "And *she's* cute, too! Let's go over and say hi. I want to meet her."

"Okay, but wait a sec—I'm almost swinging as high as you!" Carla pumped harder. "Do you think it's possible to go so high that you can loop over the bar? My brother Todd told me he knew a kid who said he did it—but I don't see how you could, really."

"I don't either," said Julie. "But it would be fun—as long as you didn't fall!"

"Wait for me!" yelled Joy, kicking her legs and straining to reach the same height.

The three girls pumped harder and flew higher until the bell rang. As she slowed her swing, Julie watched the kindergartners line up by the door. By the time she and Carla and Joy had jumped off the swings and were running toward the building, the kindergartners had gone inside.

After school Julie and Carla walked out to the playground gate together. Julie hoped Carla might invite her over to her house. She wanted to see Carla's big house—was it really nearly as big as the White House?—and meet Carla's dog, Blackjack. She wanted to see all of his tricks. It would be fun to meet Carla's family, too. But Carla didn't say anything. So Julie invited Carla to come over to her apartment instead, hoping the invitation would remind Carla that it was actually *her* turn to invite Julie.

Carla shook her head. "Sorry, I can't today. I have to go straight home to babysit for Nan and baby Debbie. And walk the dog. I'll take them all to the playground. The boys all have sports after school, or music lessons—I forget what—but they're not going to be home."

"I could help you babysit," Julie offered eagerly, "or throw a ball for the dog while you watch your sisters."

"Sorry, I'm not allowed to have friends over when my parents aren't home."

"Well, the playground isn't your house. I could meet you there."

"No, better not," said Carla. "We might just

stay home instead. It's so foggy today."

Julie shrugged. "Okay, well, I'll see you tomorrow then." She didn't see why Carla had to be so stingy with her little sisters and her dog!

Carla started up the hilly street away from her. Julie set off walking in the opposite direction, toward her own home. Maybe she'd stop at Joy's house and see if Joy wanted help with the dog-walking job.

She crossed the busy street and continued up the next block. A familiar figure came around the corner, wearing a light blue hooded jacket. It looked like Carla—but hadn't Carla just set off in the opposite direction?

"Hey, Carla!" shouted Julie, and she started running. But the figure didn't turn. Perhaps it wasn't Carla after all. Julie slowed, frowning.

It *was* Carla. She was sure of it. But if Carla had errands in Julie's neighborhood, then why hadn't she said so? Had she changed her mind about going straight home, then gone around the block and crossed the street ahead of Julie? *Maybe she just didn't hear me shout*, Julie reasoned.

She shouted Carla's name again, more loudly, but still the figure ahead of her did not stop. In fact, it walked even faster—almost as if it didn't want someone catching up.

Her curiosity piqued, Julie decided to follow. Certainly Nancy Drew and Harriet the Spy would want to know what was going on! Julie sucked in her breath, hitched up her school backpack, and started walking faster.

She shadowed Carla—if it was Carla—for two blocks, even past her own street. The backpack seemed to grow heavier and heavier with each block. Then Carla veered off toward Market Street, and Julie's steps faltered. If she went as far as Market, she'd really be going out of her way. But the neighborhood ahead wasn't entirely unfamiliar; Julie had been there once before when she'd visited the veterans' rehab center where Hank worked. Maybe she could stop in and see him, and he'd offer both her and Carla rides home. But what if Hank wasn't there?

As Julie stood there indecisively, the toot of a car horn made her jump. "Hey, babe, goin' my way?" called a familiar voice.

It was Tracy, driving Mom's station wagon. She had the window rolled down and a grin on her face. "Mom sent me on an errand! I've finished at the bank now, and there's time for ice cream. Want to hitch a ride?"

Julie watched the light blue jacket a block ahead merge into a throng of people crossing busy Market Street, and then disappear in the crowd. Ice cream with her big sister suddenly sounded like a lot more fun than playing Harriet the Spy. "It's a date!" she said. "Thanks, Tracy."

After their ice cream, Julie and Tracy arrived home to find Mom and Hank outside, building a ramp to go up the front steps leading to the apartment. "There's no way the soldiers in wheelchairs will be able to get up these steps," Joyce Albright explained to her daughters.

Hank nodded, his kind face creased with a frown. "So many buildings are not accessible to people in wheelchairs. How are they supposed to live independently if they can't even get inside most buildings in this city?"

"It's a real problem," Julie's mom agreed. "But at least our apartment is going to be accessible when we finish this ramp!"

"The ramp would also be good for getting strollers into the building, Mom," Julie pointed out.

"I guess so," her mom replied. "But nobody in the building has a stroller."

"But we *could* have one," said Julie, "if we had a little kid to push in it! Oh, Mom, I'd love to have a little sister or brother."

Hank laughed. "I think your mom has enough on her plate just raising you two girls."

"The other day you were asking for a border collie and a bigger house—and now you want another sibling?" Mom smiled ruefully at Julie.

"She wants what that new girl has," Tracy said. "That Carla." Tracy rolled her eyes and brushed past Julie on her way inside.

Julie followed. "What's wrong with that? It would be nice to have a bigger house, and a dog, and other sisters and brothers, especially if they weren't so crabby all the time!"

"Well, I'll tell you one thing Carla doesn't have," said Tracy as they opened their apartment door and went into the small, cozy living room.

"What?"

"She doesn't have two brothers at a private school called Maxwell Academy, that's what."

The hairs at the back of Julie's neck seemed to stir in a nonexistent breeze. "What are you talking about? What do you mean, Tracy?"

"I mean Tim and Tom Warner don't go to Maxwell Academy! Because—well, I wanted to meet the eleventh-grade brother, okay? And so I checked the phone books and even called information—not just for San Francisco, but for schools all over the whole Bay Area. And guess what, Julie? There's no such school by that name."

5
SECRETS

Julie left early the next morning, eager to get to school. She wanted to ask Carla about Maxwell Academy, because obviously there had been some mistake. That's what she'd told Tracy. Carla's brothers had only just started there; probably Carla had simply gotten the name wrong.

It would be fun for Tracy to meet Tom—or was it Tim? The brother in eleventh grade, anyway. Maybe Tracy would start dating him. Maybe they'd fall in love! Tracy had had several crushes that Julie knew about, but no steady boyfriend. If Tracy fell in love with Carla's brother, and they got married when they were older, then Julie and Carla would be sisters-in-law, or something. If Mom wouldn't adopt some

39

little kids, then having Carla's big family as in-laws would be the next best thing!

The bell rang just as Julie arrived, and she ran to stand in line with her class. Carla was ahead of her, talking to T. J. She smiled at Julie but continued talking to T. J. as the line moved inside and down the hallway to the classroom.

The fifth-graders hung their coats in their lockers. "Hey, Carla," Julie said as she shrugged out of her jacket. "What school do your brothers go to?"

"I already told you. Maxwell Academy." Carla raised her eyebrows. "Why?"

"Well, my sister Tracy wanted to meet your brother Tim, and so—"

"He already has a girlfriend," said Carla. "So tell your sister she'll have to look for a boyfriend somewhere else!"

"Okay, but the thing is, Tracy looked up your brothers' school—Maxwell Academy, right? And she couldn't find it listed in the phone book—"

"Listen," said Carla, grinning. "I have an idea. Tim has a good friend named Peter, and *he* doesn't have a girlfriend. So maybe we can introduce him to your sister somehow. I'll talk to Tim about it and we'll try to work something out, okay?" They pushed past the kids still hanging their coats up. "It'll be fun playing matchmaker," Carla whispered conspiratorially to Julie. She sat down at her desk.

Frowning, Julie sat at her own desk. But before she had a chance to say anything more to Carla, Mrs. Duncan motioned for silence.

"We're starting a new unit in science on molds," the teacher informed them, and some of the kids groaned. "You'll be working on this first project in groups." She assigned everyone to a group and then explained the assignment. They were to grow bread mold in different areas of the classroom and chart the molds' growth every day. Julie and T. J. were in the same group, along with a boy named Glenn who was always reading comic books when he should have been reading his textbooks, and a girl named Marina who was fluent in Spanish because her family spoke it at home.

Everyone moved around the room to sit with the people in their groups. Carla was with a group over by the windows. Julie, T. J., Glenn, and Marina sat at the front of the room together. After much discussion, they decided to put their piece of bread in the corner cabinet under the fish tank.

"It's dark in there, and sort of warm from the aquarium pump," said T. J. "I bet that'll be a great place to grow some really gross mold!"

Marina placed the slice of bread on a white paper plate and slid the plate onto the shelf. She closed the cupboard door carefully. "Okay—now we need to write down what we've done so far." She looked at Glenn. "You're the recorder, Glenn. Hey—hello? Earth to Spider Man!"

Glenn hastily shut his comic book. "What?" he asked blankly.

Julie and Marina shook their heads at him. He was impossible! "Never mind," said Julie. "I'll be the recorder." She didn't like working on projects that earned one grade for everyone in the group. Some people always ended up doing more work than others. She opened her science notebook and neatly wrote down the date and time and the location of their bread. Then she added, *Condition of bread: Fresh, soft, white.*

The classroom door opened and a little girl entered the room with a note in her hand. It was the girl Julie had seen on the playground— Carla's little sister, Nancy.

"Hey!" exclaimed Julie, turning to Carla, who crouched with her group near the windows. "Hey, Carla! There's your sister."

Carla looked up, startled.

"It's Nancy!" said Julie, pointing to where the child now stood at the teacher's desk, handing Mrs. Duncan the note.

"Who?" T. J. snorted. "That's not *Nancy.* That's Ronnie's sister, Beth!"

Julie looked over at Ronnie, who was with his group by the bulletin board. He was waving at the little girl.

She giggled and waved back. "That's my big brother," she announced to the room proudly, and the fifth-graders laughed. The teacher penned a reply and handed the note back to the little girl.

After Beth left the room, Julie walked over to Carla's group. "I don't get it, Carla. That was the girl you pointed out on the playground and said was Nancy."

"What are you talking about?" asked Carla. She appealed to her group. "Why would I do that?" She shrugged. "Ronnie's sister was probably one of the kids playing hopscotch with Nancy. You were obviously looking at the wrong girl."

"She was the one wearing the cute green hat, remember?"

Carla gazed at her blankly. "You must have been looking at a different girl, that's all."

Julie hesitated. It was on the tip of her tongue to ask about Maxwell Academy again, but Carla turned back to her group and started talking about bread mold. Julie felt her heart beating hard in her chest, as if she'd been running. She took a deep breath.

Mrs. Duncan announced it was time for their history lesson.

SECRETS

Julie sat down reluctantly, feeling unsettled. She doodled in the margin of her history notebook. Mrs. Duncan started talking about colonial times, about how Patriot spies—both men and women—used codes to send messages that the King's soldiers would not be able to understand. "A spy's job was to sniff out secrets, line up the clues, figure out the patterns, and never let the British know he or she was onto their plans."

Julie glanced over at Carla, who was staring fixedly at the board. Carla's mouth was set in a tight line. Her arms were folded across her chest. Her eyes were in shadow. She looked, Julie thought suddenly, like a person with secrets.

Julie remembered how Carla had scurried along the streets yesterday, heading to Market Street even though her home lay in the opposite direction. She'd *said* she needed to be home right after school. And Tracy had looked up a school named Maxwell Academy only to find that there wasn't one. And Julie was almost certain that Carla had pointed to Beth out on the playground yet said she was her *own* sister, Nancy.

But—what did it all mean? What was the pattern?

What secrets was Carla Warner keeping?

6
AN UNSETTLING VISIT

Every other Friday after school, when their dad's flight schedule allowed, Julie and Tracy went back to their old home for the weekend. This Friday Tracy was driving. "Turn left at the light, please," Mrs. Albright instructed. "We need to make a little detour."

"Where?" asked Tracy, putting on her turn signal. "Why?"

"We're stopping at the rehab center. Hank's got a twenty-pound turkey for me to pick up. The veterans who are coming to dinner all chipped in together to buy it."

"I'll wait in the car," Tracy said, turning the corner carefully. "I don't want to see a bunch of depressing old dudes in wheelchairs before I have to."

Mrs. Albright pressed her lips together but didn't reply. Julie was glad to keep the peace.

"I'll come in with you, Mom," Julie said hastily. "I'd like to meet the soldiers."

"Goody Two-shoes," muttered Tracy as she pulled up smoothly in front of the veterans' rehabilitation center.

"You may not be able to park here for long," Mom told Tracy. "If you're asked to move the car, please just circle around the block a few times and watch for us. We won't be long."

Julie followed her mother through the wide glass doors of the rehab center. The lobby inside was well-lit and seemed sunny even on this dreary November afternoon. Tall green plants in oversized pots stood near the windows. The receptionist behind the desk smiled at Julie and her mom. "May I help you?" she asked.

Mrs. Albright explained that they had come to pick up a turkey.

She laughed. "Oh, yes, I've heard about that bird." She turned to Julie. "Hello, dear," she said. "Welcome to rehab!"

"Hi," said Julie. The friendly woman's name-plate read *Ms. Joplin.* Julie knew that Tracy was in favor of the new title for all women. "It's better than Mrs. or Miss," Tracy insisted, "because no one can tell if a woman is married or single—and that's the way it should be, really. After all, men go by *Mr.* and nobody can tell whether *they're* married. We want equal rights!"

Ms. Albright, Julie thought to herself, liking the sound of it. That would be her name one day. Unless, of course, it was *President Albright.*

"The fellows are all down in the dayroom," Ms. Joplin was saying to Mom. "I think our red-bearded angel is with them." She winked at Julie.

I wonder if she has a crush on Hank? Julie wondered. *And if she married him, would she still be Ms.?* She followed her mom down the hallway to a large living room.

The room was brightly lit and cheerfully furnished with clusters of armchairs and more of the tall potted plants. And there were men—lots of them. A few were elderly, a few were middle-aged, but most were young. Men in wheelchairs sat watching TV or doing jigsaw puzzles at several card tables set up around the room. At one larger table, four young men were playing cards. Hank's red hair was immediately visible in a corner of the room, where he sat talking earnestly to a young soldier slumped in a wheelchair. The young man was not responding.

Hank waved when he saw Julie and her mom and came over to them. "Hello! Come meet the turkeys who will be coming to dinner!"

The men at the card table laughed and moved their chairs so that they could shake Mrs. Albright's hand. They introduced themselves: James Horner. Tubby Wolfowitz. Abe Taylor. Kenny O'Shaughnessy. They were pleased to meet Julie and her mother and were delighted to be invited to Thanksgiving dinner. "It's an honor," the man named Kenny said.

"It'll be great to get out of here and into a real home again, even for an afternoon!" said the tall, sinewy man called Tubby.

Julie was sorry to see that James and Kenny

were each missing a leg. Abe's legs were covered by a blanket, and one eye was covered by a patch. Tubby had only one arm, and the skin on his neck was puckered as if from a burn. She couldn't tell why Tubby was sitting in a wheel-chair. All of these soldiers had clearly suffered terribly in Vietnam, yet their manner was so pleasant, Julie couldn't feel sad around them. The only one who made her sad was the soldier in the corner—the young one Hank had been sitting with when they'd first walked in. He was staring across the room but looked away when Julie met his eyes.

While Mom and Hank chatted with the men who would be their guests, and Kenny rolled into the nearby kitchen to bring out the frozen turkey, Julie sidled over to the soldier in the corner. Maybe she could cheer him up.

This soldier seemed younger than the other men in the room. His hair was long and dark. He didn't look much older than the high-school boys Tracy knew. The tall one-armed soldier named Tubby was thin, but this boy looked gaunt to the point of emaciation, and his bony hands lay limply on his blue-jean-covered legs. The dark eyes that had stared across the room at Julie were now cast down at the floor. He was handsome, even though he was so skinny. He looked—more than any of the others, really—like someone who needed a Thanksgiving feast.

"Um, hi," Julie said.

He raised his head and stared blankly at her without smiling. His dark, haunted eyes seemed to stare right through Julie's head.

She took a step back, then caught herself. "I'm Julie," she said in a bright voice, holding out her hand to him.

He stared at her hand but didn't shake it. Surprised at his unfriendliness, she felt her face flush. After a moment, she put her hands behind her back.

"W-well, some of the soldiers are coming to our house for Thanksgiving. I just wondered if—um—you wanted to come, too. We'll have a lot of good food, and—"

He whirled his chair away from her to face

the window. "What's the point?" His voice was harsh and raspy, like sandpaper.

Julie caught her breath. His ingratitude felt almost like a slap. Her face still flushed and eyes stinging with hurt and embarrassment, Julie hurried back across the room to Hank and her mom, who were saying good-bye to the men. Hank carried the large turkey, well wrapped in plastic bags, out to the car for them.

"Thank you so much!" Mrs. Albright told him.

"Thank *you*," he said, setting the turkey in the trunk. "It means a lot to these guys, being invited to your home for Thanksgiving. And thank you, Julie, for taking time to talk to young Mr. Gloomy."

"*Trying* to talk to him," Julie corrected him. "But he obviously didn't want to talk to me."

"Don't take it personally. He has a lot of problems," Hank told her. "He's having a hard time and barely speaks to anyone. He refuses to go anywhere, and sometimes he won't even see his family. He won't be coming to dinner."

"Well, I mean, he could have just said no thanks. He didn't have to act like such a—such a jerk," Julie grumbled.

"What's his story?" asked Mom.

"He hasn't told us. Sometimes the guys who come here—they don't mean to act like jerks, they just don't have the right words to tell how bad they're feeling."

"I do feel sorry for him," Julie said. "For all of them."

"They don't need our pity," Hank told her gently. "They need our gratitude."

Julie and her mom said good-bye to Hank and got into the car. Tracy negotiated the rush-hour traffic competently, and soon they were pulling up in front of their old house.

Mom slid into the driver's seat and waited till the girls had stepped inside the front door before she drove away. Julie waved good-bye, and then turned to greet Dad. She knew that shuttling between their parents was the best way to stay close to both of them, but it never stopped feeling a little bit awkward.

Dad's house always felt strangely unfamiliar and completely familiar at the same time. Julie knew every nook and cranny: the curve of the handrail on the stairs, the way the light filtered in through every window, how her own bedroom window framed the best climbing tree in the neighborhood. Her bedroom still had the soft shag rug and flowered wallpaper that she had helped choose back when she was in second grade. But last year most of her bedroom furniture had been moved to the new apartment, and her old room now felt empty and barren.

At least good old Nutmeg was still here. The rabbit lived in a large cage in the backyard, but Dad had already brought him in and set him in his basket by the window. Julie stroked his soft brown fur. She was glad Ivy took care of him whenever Dad's flight schedule kept him away from home.

"May I call Ivy after dinner?" Julie asked as they sat down at the dining-room table.

"Sure," Dad said. "Maybe she'd like to go with us tomorrow morning to the farmers' market."

"Hey, wait!" Tracy protested. "What farmers' market? You said I get to take the car to Ellen's tomorrow."

"I haven't forgotten," Dad assured her as he sliced the meat loaf and slid a piece onto her plate. "The farmers' market isn't too far from here. We'll hop a bus, and you can take the car. But I want you home in time for dinner. We're going to whip up a fresh vegetable soup."

"Okay," Tracy said, then grinned. "I didn't know you knew how to cook, Dad." Most weekends at Dad's they had either meat loaf or tuna casserole, the two dishes he knew how to make. The rest of the time they went out for meals. Tracy's favorite place served Mexican food and was just around the corner. Julie liked the deli sandwiches two blocks away. And they all loved eating at the Happy Panda, Ivy's grandparents' restaurant in Chinatown.

"Well," Dad replied, "if you ladies need equal rights, then so do we men. So I've decided to learn a few new recipes."

"Good for you, Dad!" cheered Julie.

"This is a new meat-loaf recipe," their father said proudly. "What do you think of it?"

"It's good!" Julie praised him. And Tracy agreed the meal was delicious.

"I've been experimenting with all sorts of different dishes," Dad continued. "The farmers' market has a better selection than the grocery stores. We'll go first thing after breakfast."

Julie ate her dinner, looking around the dining room where her whole family had eaten countless meals together. The table was big enough to seat eight comfortably, and several more chairs could be pulled up as needed. Julie pictured the little table in their apartment. How would they manage to fit all their Thanksgiving guests around it—especially all those men in wheelchairs?

"Dad, you'll be away for Thanksgiving, right?" asked Julie suddenly. "You won't get any turkey!"

"That's right. I'll be flying to Germany. But you can bet the stewardesses will be serving our passengers a Thanksgiving meal, right there in their seats! I'm sure they'll bring me a plate, too."

But Julie was less concerned with her dad's turkey dinner than with the one they'd be sharing with Hank's Vietnam vets. She'd just thought of a wonderful plan. They could have the feast *here*. "Dad, could we use this house while you're away?" she asked eagerly. "Just for the Thanksgiving feast? Mom's inviting all these wounded soldiers, and I don't think we'll have enough room in the apartment, and I thought maybe—"

Dad smiled. "If your mom wants to talk to me about that idea, I'll be happy to listen."

Tracy snorted.

"Vietnam veterans, you say?" asked Dad.

"Yes, they're men that Hank works with at the rehab center," Julie explained. "You remember Hank, right?"

"Yes, I've met him," her dad replied. "The red-haired fellow."

"He's a Vietnam vet himself, and he works at the rehab center on Market Street."

"I wonder if the center needs some crutches," Daniel Albright said musingly. "I've got an old pair in the closet, from the time I broke my leg."

"You fell off the porch roof," Julie remembered. "You were cleaning gutters."

"And my foot slipped," said Dad.

"We were so worried," said Tracy.

Dad smiled. "Well, luckily I'm fine, and I still have those crutches. Maybe they'll come in useful for some other guys who have had close calls, too. I'm happy to donate them."

"Thanks, Dad," said Julie. "I'll tell Hank."

That night Julie dreamed about Carla. In the dream she and Carla were hobbling through Golden Gate Park on crutches, side by side. Then the boy in the wheelchair, the one with the haunted eyes, rolled up to them. He held a beautiful black and white border collie by a leash. "Here," he said in his raspy voice, holding the leash out to Julie. "He's yours if you want him." And Julie did want him—*so* much—and she struggled to hold the leash and maneuver on the crutches, but the crutches kept falling, and the leash kept dropping—and the dog ran off.

And then she woke up, and it was morning. She found her dad downstairs in the kitchen making scrambled eggs. She sat at the table sipping her orange juice, remembering the joy she'd felt in the dream with that leash firmly held in her hand—before everything started falling apart. The boy's raspy voice echoed in her head.

After breakfast, Tracy drove off in their dad's blue sedan. Julie and Dad watched the car disappear around the corner. "Almost grown-up," Dad said, squeezing Julie's shoulder. "Don't you grow up on me," he added with a smile.

"Not too fast," Julie agreed. "Oh, look, here's Poison Ivy!" She ran to meet her best friend, who was just crossing the street.

"Hey, Alley-Oop!" Ivy greeted Julie. "I missed you." Ivy's thick black hair moved like a curtain as she hugged Julie. "Where's Tracy going? I saw her driving away."

Julie explained that her sister was going to see a friend in Oakland. "Just think—someday you and I will be driving back and forth to visit each other."

"That'll be fun." Ivy smiled at Julie. "So, what's up? It's been dullsville around here all week. Tons of homework every night, and lots of extra gymnastics practice because I've got a meet coming up next month. What about you?"

"It's been a strange week, actually," Julie said slowly. "I've made a new friend—I think."

"You *think?*"

"Well, Carla's sometimes a little bit . . . odd." Julie told Ivy all about the new girl. "I do like her a lot," she finished. "I just can't figure her out."

"She sounds nice," said Ivy.

"She *is* nice," Julie agreed. "But I get the feeling she's keeping secrets." She chose her words with care. "I mean, she's lots of fun, but she's also *mysterious.*"

"You and your mysteries!" laughed Ivy.

Julie smiled back at her friend. But the dream image of Carla hobbling on crutches flashed in Julie's mind, and she couldn't quite manage a laugh.

7
THE OGRE

"All right, girls!" Mr. Albright called as he locked the front door. "Ready to go?"

Julie, Ivy, and Dad walked two blocks to the bus stop and then caught the bus to the farmers' market. The November day was damp and cool, but for a change the sun shone brightly. The market was a cluster of stalls set up on both sides of the street, which had been closed to traffic. Julie and Ivy were lured to the enticing displays of autumn fruits and vegetables, cheese and nuts, braided ropes of garlic, handmade bread rolls, cakes, and pastries. They eyed the shiny pumpkins, gourds, and squashes. Dad went from stall to stall, picking out cabbages and leeks, beans and apples. Julie and Ivy sampled slices of apples or chunks of cheese whenever they were offered. "Most fresh-air markets close in October," Dad told the girls. "But this one stays open long enough for people to do their Thanksgiving shopping." He added to his bag some carrots and two large yellow onions.

"I wish you were going to be home for Thanksgiving," Julie told him.

He put an arm around her shoulders and gave her a quick hug. "I'll be thinking of you enjoying your turkey as I'm flying off to Germany," he replied with a laugh. "But a leftover piece of pumpkin pie will be greatly appreciated."

"I'll save you a slice—" Julie promised, then broke off at the sight of a familiar face at the stall across the street. "Hey, there's Carla! That's the girl I was telling you about, Ivy. Come with me, I'll introduce you. We'll be right back, Dad!"

Julie started across the crowded street to a stall piled with orange pumpkins and yellow squashes and green apples in wooden crates. A banner stretched from pole to pole, announcing *Earthlight Farm*. "Hey, Carla!" she called.

Carla was filling a basket with apples from a large box. She turned in surprise, then hurried away from the stall, coming toward them. "Hi, Julie," she said, wiping her hands on the green bib apron she wore. The apron had the Earthlight logo—a white sunburst with the name of the farm—on a big pocket in front. "What are you doing here?"

"Shopping with my dad." Then Julie introduced Ivy. "This is my best friend, Ivy Ling. We used to be neighbors until I moved to our apartment. Now I mostly see her on weekends. I was just telling her about you!"

"Hi, Ivy," Carla said. She glanced over her shoulder at the stall. "Um, I can't really talk now."

"Do you actually work here?" Julie asked.

"Come over here where we can talk for a minute," Carla said, linking arms with Julie on one side and Ivy on the other. She maneuvered them away from her stall and around the side of a blue pickup truck with the Earthlight Farm logo on the side. "I do work here—just on the weekends. You know, for a little mad money."

"How did you get a real job?" asked Julie, impressed.

"Well, my parents are friends with the company's owner, so he lets me help out. My parents think it's a good idea for us kids to earn some of our own spending money—even though they give us a pretty good allowance."

"That's so cool!" said Ivy. "I wish I could have a job. My grandparents have a restaurant in Chinatown, and they said they'll hire me when I'm sixteen. But that's forever to wait!"

Julie glanced over her shoulder at the Earthlight stall. A woman wearing a green apron like Carla's stood behind the wooden table. She was waving and beckoning to them.

"Hey, somebody wants you," Julie said, pointing.

"Yeah, I'd better get back to work," said Carla, "or the boss will fire me."

Julie looked closer. The tall, thin woman with the limp dark ponytail seemed familiar somehow ... but where would she have seen her before? Julie stood, forehead creased in a frown, and a memory flashed through her mind.

"Hey!" she exclaimed. "She was outside in the rain last weekend, rooting through the trash on our street. She stole something right out of our trash can!"

"That's weird," said Ivy. "Why would she do that?"

"It must have been somebody else," said Carla, shrugging. "Anyway, I have to go."

"We'll come with you," said Julie. "Let's ask your boss if she'll hire us, too!" It would be so fun, Julie thought, to work on the weekends and earn some spending money. After all, the holidays were coming up fast. Of course she'd have to ask her parents, but if they knew the Earthlight owner was a friend of Carla's family, surely it would be fine.

"No!" said Carla. "Stay away from the stall." She reached out and grabbed Julie's arm. "Don't go over there. That woman—she's an ogre!"

"An *ogre?*" Julie stared at Carla. "But we wanted to ask about getting jobs, too. Then we could all work together. It would be fun."

"Well, ask somewhere else. Just stay away from Earthlight." Carla's voice shook with intensity. She pulled them back behind the pickup truck and ducked low. "Listen! That woman I work for—you've got to watch out for her. I mean it, she could be dangerous."

"What do you mean?" asked Julie.

"She—she's a crook!"

Julie and Ivy gasped. "A *crook?*"

Carla pulled them lower behind the truck so that they were crouching by the curb. "Okay, she probably *was* the person you saw digging through the trash. I'm not supposed to talk about it. But I've been watching her for some time." She lowered her voice to a whisper. "We're setting a trap."

"A *trap?*" A shiver of excitement tickled Julie's shoulder blades.

Ivy stood up, her hands on her hips. "Who's *we?* What's going on?"

Carla looked apprehensively over her shoulder, then spoke in a low, hurried voice. "All right,

I'll tell you what's really going on, but you have to promise not to breathe a word of it."

"We promise!" Julie and Ivy said together.

"Her name's Barb. She's . . . a thief. But I can't let on that I know. It could be dangerous."

"Well, the things she was taking on our street were already in the trash," Julie said. "So I'm not sure it was really against the law."

"No, it's more than that. She—she's been stealing from the company. From Earthlight! Not just a few pieces of fruit—but money from the head office. Embezzling their money!"

Julie edged along so that she could peer around the back of the truck. She could see the woman waiting on a customer. Her straggly ponytail hung limply and her smile seemed pasted on.

"You shouldn't keep working for her if she's a criminal," Ivy exclaimed, looking worried.

"You'd better call the police. Or at least tell your parents," advised Julie.

"Oh—my parents know already. The owner of Earthlight is a guy named Mr. Anderson. He asked my dad to look into this case. He's a detective, and I'm sort of helping him. But I'm not supposed to tell anyone, so please pretend I never said a word!"

"But isn't your dad a doctor?" Julie felt puzzled.

"Yes—well, he *was*. But he isn't anymore. He's semi-retired now, in order to work with the F.B.I. We just keep saying he's a doctor—that's his cover." Carla glanced over her shoulder. Julie looked, too, and saw the woman, hands on hips and a frown on her face, scanning the crowded street. Looking for Carla? The hair at the back of Julie's neck prickled.

"Anyway, I'm helping him," Carla said. "I have to keep my eye on the thief."

"So *that* must have been what you were doing Thursday after school," Julie blurted out. "I mean, you told me you had to go straight home to take care of your sisters, but then I saw you heading toward Market Street . . ."

Carla stared at her. Then she lowered her voice further and leaned close. "Yes, I was trying to track down a clue for my dad." She reached for Julie's hand and squeezed it. "I've got to go now," she murmured. "I need to get back to work." She darted out from behind the pickup and hurried back to the stall.

Ivy's eyes were big. "A dad who works for the F.B.I.—and a chance to work with him catching criminals—whoa!" she said. "She's like Nancy Drew!"

"Carla is *so* lucky," agreed Julie as she and Ivy headed back across the street to find Julie's dad. "She has the most exciting life. All *I* ever do is homework and chores . . . and fight with my sister."

"*And* hang out on weekends with your best friend," Ivy reminded her. "Don't forget that."

Laughing, they started up the street, where they could see Julie's dad standing near a stall selling fresh fruit pies. Pilots were cool—but not nearly as cool as detectives, Julie thought. She felt a stab of envy that Carla, who had everything, also had a real mystery to work on. Maybe she and Ivy could help Carla solve this case!

THE OGRE

Suddenly Ivy clutched Julie's arm and whirled her around. "Oh no, *look!*"

Julie stared back down the street at the Earthlight Farm stall, where Carla and the woman named Barb stood facing each other. Barb's expression looked angry as she spoke to Carla. She held a short, sharp knife in her hand—and pointed it straight at Carla.

8
VISIT TO A PAINTED LADY

"That woman is threatening her," Ivy whispered. "We'd better get help!"

But before they could run to Julie's dad or summon a policeman, the woman moved behind the stall again and started serving her customers, tossing apples into a paper sack with quick, angry movements. Carla looked up the street and saw Julie and Ivy watching. She gestured for them to go away. Then she started helping customers too.

Would Carla welcome their help, or was she handling things just fine on her own? After all, she didn't look scared now, Julie noted. Just *tense*.

How much danger was Carla in, trying to trap the woman she called an *ogre*?

"Don't you think we should tell the police?" Ivy asked.

"Her dad *is* the police," Julie reminded her. "Or at least he's working with the F.B.I." She watched Carla across the crowded street. "I think Carla can probably handle it. She wouldn't like us getting in the way. But let's come back tomorrow and see what's going on. We can sort of shadow Carla to see what happens with that woman."

"You mean, we'll shadow Carla while she's investigating Barb?"

"Right. We'll work undercover—like Carla and her dad. Just to keep an eye on Carla and make sure she's safe. And we'll call the police right away if we see anything else suspicious."

With that plan decided, the girls went back home with Julie's father. They helped him cut up fresh vegetables for the soup and then went upstairs to Julie's bedroom.

Julie put on a record, and then she and Ivy built a maze for Nutmeg from empty cardboard boxes. "Look, it's a puzzle for you, Nutmeg,"

Julie said, coaxing her rabbit out of his cage. "Can you find the treat?" It took a while, but the little rabbit seemed happy to wander the maze until he found the carrot at the center.

Julie cuddled her pet and stroked Nutmeg's soft fur. "You're almost as clever as a border collie," she whispered into one of the rabbit's silken ears.

That night, Julie couldn't stop thinking about the events of the past few days. She lay in bed, watching the lights of passing cars make patterns on her wall. The bedroom lay deep in shadow. In the near-darkness, her sleepover duffel bag looked a bit like a border collie. Her desk chair looked like a wheelchair—with the slumped figure of the dark-eyed soldier in it. Her tall lamp by the bookcase looked like the ogre ... Julie shivered and turned over so that she was facing the wall.

At last she slept, but it was not a refreshing

sleep. She woke up on Sunday morning feeling as if she'd been wandering through a maze all night, hitting dead ends at every turn, with no clever rabbit to lead the way out.

Julie went downstairs and found her dad at the kitchen table, reading the newspaper.

"Hi, pumpkin," he greeted her. "You're up early. Want to help me make pancakes and bacon?"

"Yum!"

As Julie was setting the platter of pancakes on the table, Tracy clattered down the stairs. "I smell something amazing," she greeted them. "And, believe me, I'm going to need sustenance, since I have to spend the *whole* day studying for my math test." She crossed her eyes at Julie. "Just wait till you're in high school."

"But I love math," Julie said. Tracy rolled her eyes in response.

"Want me to quiz you?" asked Dad.

"Oh, would you?" Tracy perked up. "That would be great."

"While you guys are doing math, can I go

back to the farmers' market with Ivy?" Julie asked. "We wanted to meet Carla there and hang out for a while."

"Take your bikes," Dad suggested. "That way you'll be home in time for lunch. Who thinks it's time to visit the Happy Panda again?"

Julie and Tracy both punched their hands high into the air. "We do, we do," they cheered. Julie stole a glance at her sister and smiled. It felt good to agree with Tracy about something.

After breakfast Julie phoned her friend. "Hi, Poison Ivy! Are you ready to check on Carla? We have to be back by one o'clock so we can go out to lunch at our favorite Chinese restaurant. You know which one I mean, Ivy—and you have to come, too, and surprise your grandparents!"

"They *will* be surprised, because I was just there on Friday with my own family," Ivy replied with a laugh.

While she waited for Ivy to arrive, Julie washed up the breakfast dishes. Then she and Ivy rode off for the farmers' market.

The journey up and down the hilly streets of

Visit to a Painted Lady

San Francisco took them quite a while, but the day was sunny and the air felt fresh. Arriving at the market, they locked their bikes to a chain-link fence on the corner and set off among the market stalls on foot. Julie saw immediately that the tall, thin woman named Barb was not at the Earthlight Farm stall. A bearded young man was slicing apples and setting them on a tray for customers to sample. There was no sign of Carla.

"Let's ask that guy where she is," Ivy suggested.

"No, wait—we don't want her to know we're checking up on her. If Carla's not with Barb, then she's obviously not in danger from her right now, so I really think we shouldn't say anything." Julie hesitated as a scary thought occurred to her: Maybe Carla and Barb *were* together right now—and Carla *was* in danger.

"But Carla did say she worked on Sunday," Ivy reminded her. "So maybe she just hasn't arrived yet. Let's wait a while and check back."

"Okay. I know—let's wait at the candy store," suggested Julie with a grin.

Together they crossed the street and headed down the block to Randy's Candies on the next corner. Suddenly Julie grabbed Ivy's hand and pulled her into an alleyway.

"What?" whispered Ivy.

"It's Barb—she was coming right up the street toward us!"

"I didn't see her," Ivy protested, shaking loose from Julie's tight grip.

"She was down by Kitchenworld, looking through the trash. I'm sure it was her."

Silent now, the girls crept to the end of the alley and peered around the building. Yes, it was Barb, about four shops down, bent so low over the metal trash bin at the curb that her head was nearly inside it. She pulled something out of the bin and stood up again. In her hand was a lidless metal saucepan. Its bottom was burned black, but Barb opened her backpack and shoved it inside. Then she looked up and saw the girls.

They turned and ran down the alley and around a corner. Panting, they clutched each other. "She saw us!" gasped Ivy.

"But at least we know she isn't hurting Carla right now," Julie said grimly. "Let's wait a few more minutes and then check the farmers' market again to see if Carla's there yet."

They took a longer route, walking several blocks and then looping back to the outdoor market. It was busier already. The air was scented with autumn bouquets at a stall called Flora-Bella. Light, happy music from two street musicians playing a violin and a flute would have made Julie's feet feel like dancing along the street— except that she was looking anxiously over at the Earthlight stall. There was no sign of the bearded man, and no sign of Carla. *Thank goodness for that*, thought Julie as she spotted Barb in the stall. Barb was already at work, the green apron around her waist, slicing apples. As they approached, she looked up—right at them, knife in hand.

"Alley-Oop," whispered Ivy, "she's creepy."

"Let's get out of here," Julie replied in a low voice. Her heart was beating hard. She and Ivy turned away. They walked as fast as they could back toward Randy's Candies, and even though

Julie knew Barb was safely at the Earthlight stall, she felt the back of her neck prickle as if someone was watching them—or following them. *I won't look back*, she told herself, and walked faster.

As they were about to enter the candy store, Julie saw a girl walking down the street on the next block, holding the leash of a black-and-white dog. "Hey, there's Carla now!" Julie cried. She darted across the street, but Ivy held back. Although she had two cats at home, dogs—especially big ones—made Ivy nervous.

"Carla said he's well trained," Julie called back to her friend. "Come on, Ivy!" Then she ran over to Carla. "Hi! We were looking for you at the market." She held out her hand to the dog, who sniffed it and wagged his silky fringed tail. He had soft brown eyes and a wet, cold nose. *What a beauty*, she thought longingly.

Ivy approached slowly, keeping behind Julie.

"Sit!" Carla commanded, and the dog obediently sat, his tail sweeping back and forth on the sidewalk.

"We saw your ogre," Julie reported.

"She was looking through the garbage," Ivy added. "Stole a pot."

Carla's face reddened. "Just keep away from her," she said in a low, tense voice. "Don't go near her."

"We didn't!" said Ivy.

There was an awkward silence.

Julie stroked the dog's soft head. "He's gorgeous," she said brightly. "Hi, boy! He does tricks, right?"

"Yes." Carla relaxed. She pointed a finger at him and commanded, "Beg, Jack!" The dog obediently sat on his haunches, paws in the air. "Good boy!"

Julie rubbed his silky ears. "Such a smart boy!" She scratched under his chin. "Let's see his other tricks."

"Well . . ." Carla hesitated. "Jack's had a long walk. I should take him home now."

"Can we come home with you—and see Jack's tricks?" Julie pressed.

"Well . . . I can show you on that patch of

grass." Carla led the dog over to a small lawn in front of a bank. She unclipped Jack's leash. He waited expectantly, staring at Carla with intelligent eyes. "Okay, watch this. Jack—roll over! Roll over, boy!"

Jack lay down and flipped over.

"Good dog!" cheered Julie and Ivy. Ivy reached out a finger to touch Jack's head.

The dog seemed to be smiling, as if he loved doing tricks for an audience. With Carla calling out the cues, he obediently danced, barked, jumped, and played dead.

Julie was impressed. "I wish my rabbit had tricks like that up her sleeve."

"He's smart!" Ivy bravely rubbed Jack's ears. "How old is he?"

"Three," said Carla. "We got him when he was a pup, and I taught him everything myself." She clipped the leash back onto Jack's leather collar. "I'd better go. See you!"

"Wait, we'll walk home with you," said Julie. She and Ivy fell into step with Carla.

"Um, I have things I have to do—"

"Chores?" Ivy sighed. "Tell me about it. I know they're waiting for me, too, this afternoon."

"Yes, chores, and I've got to take care of the baby while my mom and dad go to one of my brother's football games."

"We could hang out with you for a while, and help with the baby and stuff," offered Julie.

"No, that's okay. I'm not supposed to have friends over while I'm babysitting. Thanks anyway." Carla seemed eager to be off and jogged away from them with Jack leading the way.

Julie grabbed Ivy's hand and sped after Carla. "Please, Carla? I've never seen your house. Just let us come with you—we won't stay."

"And I need the exercise," said Ivy. "My gymnastics coach is always after our team to get out and walk or jog."

Carla seemed resigned to their presence. She asked about Ivy's gymnastics team, and Ivy told her all about the tournament she was training for.

Julie piped up, "Ivy is so amazing, Carla!

You'll have to come and watch one of the meets. I think she's going to end up an Olympic medalist someday. I really do!"

"I've never done gymnastics," said Carla. "But my little sister is just starting."

"May I hold Jack's leash?" Julie asked, and she felt a thrill when Carla handed it to her.

After a few more blocks, they turned onto a steep street of large Victorian houses. Julie was puffing slightly by the time they reached the top, but the dog pranced at her side without any effort at all.

Carla stopped in front of a tall, narrow three-story green house with white and blue trim, a front porch, and a round tower. "This is it."

"Such a pretty house," Ivy said. "And such a huge hill!"

The dog bounded up onto the porch. Carla took a frayed towel from an umbrella stand next to the front door and carefully wiped his paws.

"Can we come in?" asked Julie. "I'd love to see that tower room! Who gets to sleep in it? I'd sure choose it for my bedroom, if I lived here!"

"It's my dad's study," said Carla. "Totally off limits, sorry."

"That's okay." Julie was eager to see the rest of the house. The front door had a blue, green, and gold stained-glass window. From the porch she could see the San Francisco Bay in the distance, sunlight glinting on sparkling water.

Ivy looked at her watch. "We'll have to hurry, Julie, if we're going to get back for lunch. It's a long walk, and then we still have to bike home from the market."

"But downhill will be faster. Let's just have a quick peek," pressed Julie.

"Okay, just for a sec." Carla pulled a key out of her pocket and unlocked the front door with its pane of colored glass. "My mom and dad aren't home just now," she said. "They've taken the baby to the park. I'll be babysitting for her later, when they get home. And Nancy is at her friend's house. And my brothers are at football practice."

"That's okay," said Julie. "We can meet them another time. But—oh, I love your house! It's really neato!" The dog pushed past her into the house, and trotted into the kitchen. They could hear him lapping up water from his bowl.

"Well, I guess you guys can look around," said Carla. "Living room, dining room, kitchen—it's just a house. But a big one!"

"I love all the stained glass," said Ivy.

"Can we see your room?" asked Julie.

"Oh—it's such a mess." Carla's laugh was shrill. "I'll show you next time."

Julie looked around the large front hallway with interest, and then stepped into the gracious living room. The warm wood of the mantel gleamed, and the silver candlesticks sparkled. Tall windows at the front and side of the house let shafts of sunlight fall across the Oriental rug. Jack ambled back into the room, jumped up onto the window seat, and curled into a ball. He seemed to watch Julie as she made her way through the rooms.

It was such a pretty house! And so clean! Carla's messy bedroom certainly didn't match the rest of the house, because every place looked perfectly tidy. There were none of the piles of papers and magazines, books and games that filled Julie's apartment.

"Oh, look—it's Jack as a puppy!" Julie stopped in front of an end table on which a vase of fresh flowers stood next to a framed photograph. She picked up the photo and looked at the laughing, silver-haired woman holding a small border collie in her arms. "Who's the lady?"

"My—my grandmother." Carla's voice was hushed. "She died."

"Where are the toys kept?" asked Ivy, standing at the foot of the staircase, one hand on the banister.

"Oh—up in the playroom." Carla's giggle sounded forced. "We have to keep things off the floor so the baby doesn't put them in her mouth. Or so Jack doesn't chew on them—Oh *no!*" Carla broke off and stared, ashen-faced, out the front window.

Julie turned and looked. A gray-haired man was striding up the path to the porch.

"Don't let him see you!" gasped Carla. "You have to get out of here. *Now!*"

9

A Sticky Web

Jack jumped down and ran to the door, tail wagging.

"*Hurry!*" Looking panicked, Carla grabbed Julie and Ivy by their arms and pulled them through the dining room, through the kitchen.

Julie could hear keys jingling in the front hall and heard the murmur of a man's voice quieting the dog.

Carla fumbled desperately to open the back door, fairly shoving the girls through it. "I'm not supposed to have visitors unless I've checked with my dad first," she hissed at them in a ragged whisper. "You've got to *go!*"

"Okay, okay—good-bye!" Julie whispered, as she followed Ivy out the back door and jumped down the wooden steps into the yard.

A Sticky Web

Julie and Ivy hid in the shadow of a large bush, pressing against the wall of the house. Julie's heart was thumping hard, as if she had just escaped terrible danger. But why was Carla so afraid of her own father? What would he do to Carla if they were caught?

The sun slipped behind a cloud and the tangled black branches that reached over the back porch suddenly looked like a net—or a web. Julie shivered. "Come on, Ivy, let's get out of here."

Cautiously they circled around through the side yard, keeping away from the windows so Carla's father wouldn't see them if he chanced to look out. Quietly Julie lifted the latch on the gate, and they slipped through to the front. Then she clutched Ivy's arm and pulled her to an abrupt stop. Carla and her father were standing on the porch, talking in low voices. He handed her something—a flash of green—that she shoved into the pocket of her jacket. She jumped down the steps to the sidewalk and then turned back and waved to him.

"Did you see that?" Julie breathed the words into Ivy's ear. "That was a wad of money!"

They waited silently until Carla's father had gone back inside the house and shut the door. Then they ran out the gate to the sidewalk. They could see Carla, already heading down the hill. Julie was about to run after Carla, but something about the way Carla glanced furtively over her shoulder as she raced down the steep street away from them made Julie pause.

Where was Carla going so fast? Why was she looking back over her shoulder as if she was afraid of someone? Was she afraid that her father was following her? But that didn't make sense. Just as the answer surfaced in Julie's mind, Ivy spoke it. "She's acting kind of like she thinks we might follow her."

Julie nodded as Carla disappeared around the corner. "But why? It's all so weird."

"Maybe not," said practical Ivy. "You're always thinking everything is a mystery. Maybe he's just sending her to the store for a gallon of milk or something. Or maybe he's sending her on some secret mission for that case they're working on."

"Yeah," said Julie, her voice uncertain. "Maybe." All the secrets Carla was keeping made Julie feel dizzy.

Sunday night Tracy drove them back to their apartment in Dad's car. The girls kissed him good-bye. "Happy Thanksgiving," Julie told Dad, hugging him hard.

"Happy Thanksgiving to both of my sweet little turkeys," Dad said. Even Tracy laughed. Her mood seemed a lot better than in the past week, Julie reflected. The way to her sister's heart was definitely through *cars*.

The girls went inside. Tracy floated off to catch up on last-minute homework. Mom and Hank were seated at the table making a list of things still needed for the Thanksgiving feast on Thursday. Julie told them about her idea that they should have the holiday feast at their old house. "There's a lot more room," Julie pointed out. "And Dad said it would be fine with him."

Hank looked interested, but Julie's mother shook her head. "No, honey. When I entertain friends, I want it to be here. Where I live now— not where I used to live."

Julie hesitated, wanting to argue her case, but Hank caught her eye and shook his head gently. She shrugged. "Well, okay, it was just a thought."

"It was nice of your dad to offer," Hank said.

Julie felt better when she saw Mom nodding in agreement. "He said he has some crutches he can donate to the rehab center, if you want them," Julie told Hank.

"We do want them!" Hank assured Julie. "And if you give me his phone number, I'll call to thank him, and arrange to pick them up after the holiday weekend."

Julie made a peanut butter sandwich and took it to her bedroom. She watched her spider in the window, illuminated by the streetlamp below. Harriet the Spy-der had spun a large web and was busy wrapping up a hapless fly.

"Enjoy your dinner," Julie told the spider. She always missed Nutmeg most after visiting Dad. But Nutmeg would be well cared for by Ivy while Dad was gone, she reminded herself. Ivy had promised to give the rabbit extra celery and carrots in honor of the holiday. And maybe even a tiny taste of pumpkin pie.

Julie thought about Carla's talented dog. Would Carla's father carve their Thanksgiving turkey and save the scraps for Jack?

The thought of Carla's father and that scary moment when he'd come home unexpectedly made Julie's heart pound again. Carla had been so frantic for them to leave! Why was she so afraid of her father?

Julie decided she would talk to Carla at school tomorrow and ask her about all the strange things that didn't make sense. Maxwell Academy. The kindergarten girl named Beth who was not Carla's sister Nancy. Why Barb at the farmers' market had threatened her with a knife. Why Carla was so terrified when her father came home. Julie sensed that all of these mysteries were pieces of a puzzle, but she couldn't see how they all fit together.

However, Carla was not in school the next day. So Julie decided she would go to Carla's house. She asked Mrs. Duncan to give her Carla's homework so that she could take it to Carla. Surely Carla's father wouldn't object to someone coming to the house on such an errand.

Would he?

It was such a long way that Julie decided to save her snack money for a bus. Before she left school, she went to the office and used the phone to call her mom.

"Gladrags—how can I help you?" Julie's mom answered in a cheerful, professional voice.

"Hi, Mom, it's me," Julie said. "Is it all right if I go to Carla's house after school? I want to take her her homework because she was out sick today."

"That's sweet of you, honey," said Mom. "But don't stay to play. It gets dark so early now, and I want you home before dark."

Julie promised she would be home before

dark and set off for the bus stop. The bus was full of high school kids, and Julie had to stand. Beside her, Julie noticed a tall, dark-haired boy who looked about Tracy's age. "Hey, Tom!" he called. "Did you get the math homework?"

Another boy waved a mimeographed sheet of paper above the heads of all the passengers. "Got it! Thanks, Timothy."

Tom? And Timothy? Julie studied the boys carefully. Could these be Carla's brothers? Her brother Tim was Tracy's age, Julie remembered. And Tom was Carla's twin. This boy next to her looked too old to be in fifth grade.

Julie considered whether to say something— maybe she could ask the boy if he had a sister named Carla—but the bus stopped with a screech of brakes, and both boys surged off with a crowd of other teenagers. Julie sighed. She rode to the next stop and then started climbing the big hill to Carla's house. Funny that Carla lived so far away from their school, Julie reflected.

The hill seemed even steeper than before, and

Julie's backpack—laden with Carla's books as well as Julie's own—grew heavier with each step. But finally she was there, standing in front of the pretty green painted lady. She walked boldly up the porch steps to the front door and pushed the doorbell.

She could hear Jack barking. She waited, but no one came to the door. She knocked, pounding loudly, and the door opened by itself. Jack bounded forward and wriggled with pleasure. "Hi, boy! Good boy! Where's Carla?"

She waited on the porch, but no one came. Jack stood with her on the porch, tail sweeping back and forth. After another minute, Julie slowly stepped into the front hallway. "Hello?" she called. "Carla?"

Carla was probably sleeping, since she was sick, Julie figured. The other kids weren't home from school yet, and her dad was probably at work, and maybe her mom had taken the baby out for a walk in the stroller. Maybe they hadn't closed the door all the way, so it hadn't latched properly. She closed it carefully behind her.

"Hello, Carla?"

Julie ventured farther into the house, through the front hall to the living room, with Jack at her side. "Carla?" she called again. She hated to wake Carla. Maybe she should just leave the schoolbooks and homework assignment sheet on the kitchen table.

In the kitchen, a cardboard box sat on the table, full of squashes, carrots, potatoes, and turnips. The logo on the side of the box caught Julie's eye: a sunburst with the words *Earthlight Farm.* "Carla?" Julie called, but not as loudly as before. "Where are you?"

Next to the box lay a wooden cutting board, with a carrot cut into sticks. Julie frowned. Something was missing. Where was the sharp knife that had cut the carrot?

The missing knife made Julie feel uneasy. She remembered the way Barb, the ogre, had brandished the knife at the Earthlight stall—how she had pointed it right at Carla.

The silence of the big house closed around her. She could hear the ticking of a clock somewhere nearby. Where was her new friend? Was Carla in danger?

Nancy Drew would not hesitate to investigate, Julie knew. Nor would Harriet the Spy. Taking a deep breath, Julie decided she would go upstairs and just peek into Carla's room to reassure herself that her friend was okay. If Carla was asleep, Julie would just leave the homework. But if the ogre was in the house, and if she had a knife . . . Carla would need help.

Julie moved into the hallway. She put her foot on the first step of the staircase.

10
CAUGHT!

Julie climbed the stairs soundlessly. Jack walked next to her, nudging her hand with his cold nose. His toenails clicked on the polished wooden floor of the upstairs hallway. "Carla?" Julie called quietly. Late-afternoon sunlight filtered in through a window at the end of the long hallway. Julie peeked into the first of the four bedrooms. It was a large room with a neatly made double bed covered in a dark blue bedspread. Probably Carla's parents' room. The next bedroom had twin beds with dark mahogany frames and a matching dresser. *Some of the boys must sleep here*, Julie thought to herself, but where was their *stuff*? She'd never met kids with such spic-and-span rooms before.

Three more doors left; one must lead to

Carla's bedroom. The first door revealed a bathroom. The second room was furnished as a study, with an old-fashioned rolltop desk and a leather chair. The last room was a storage room, full of stacked cardboard boxes. Perplexed, Julie bent down to read the labels scrawled in black ink.

Jane—dresses, said one. *Jane—books,* said another. *Jane—family photos.*

Julie straightened up. Who was Jane? Julie didn't recall a Warner sister named Jane. Could Jane be Carla's grandmother who had died?

Julie frowned. Where was Carla's room? Come to think of it, where was the baby's room? Julie hadn't seen a crib in the master bedroom. And hadn't Carla told Ivy that the playroom was upstairs?

Julie walked down the hallway and opened the last two doors. One was a linen closet. The other revealed a completely empty closet with buttons on the wall. *Oh!* thought Julie, blinking with sudden realization. *It's an elevator!*

How intriguing that Carla's house had an elevator. Julie stepped inside. There had to be bedrooms downstairs that Julie hadn't noticed. Maybe Carla was fast asleep in her bedroom downstairs. "Come on, Jack!" she urged the black-and-white dog, but he just sat in the hallway, wagging his tail. She felt that the friendly tail was a good sign; surely he would not wag it if Carla were in danger?

Julie looked closely at the buttons inside the elevator. *Light* said the first one. *Up* said another. *Down* said yet another. Simple enough.

Julie pushed the *light* button, and a light turned on in the elevator. She pushed the *down* button. As the elevator door slid soundlessly closed, Jack dashed for the stairs, his nails scrabbling on the wood.

In seconds the elevator door slid open again, and Julie found herself facing a closed wooden door. She turned the knob, and the door opened to reveal Jack, sitting waiting, his tail sweeping the floor like a plume.

"Good boy," she said, pushing off the *light* button and stepping out of the elevator. Now, where in the world was Carla?

Julie followed the dog. He ran through the formal dining room, then through the elegant living room, and then stopped by the front door and sat, tail wagging. She heard footsteps on the porch.

Julie flushed with embarrassment as the front door opened and Carla's dad stepped in.

The dog ran to him, but Carla's dad just stared at Julie, his bushy gray eyebrows drawing together in a frown. "Who in the world are you?" he demanded. "And what are you doing here?"

For a second Julie's tongue seemed to stick to the roof of her mouth. "Um—hello," she managed. "I'm sorry to have come in—the door was open and I was just stopping by to—"

"It was open?" He looked even more annoyed. "Carla must not have shut it tightly."

"Well, I know I shouldn't have gone in, but I thought Carla was home, and I wanted to bring her—"

Carla's father suddenly interrupted her. "Oh, yes," he said with a smile. "The order of Girl

Scout cookies. But I have to warn you, I won't be ordering any more this year. The last batch was delicious, but I must have gained ten pounds!"

Julie relaxed. "Oh, no," she said, returning his smile. "I'm not selling anything. I was just bringing Carla's homework."

He looked puzzled.

"Because she's sick," Julie continued. "I mean, isn't she? The teacher said I should bring her the assignments . . ." Her voice trailed off at his expression.

"Carla?" he asked. "Carla's homework?"

"Yes. She wasn't at school, so I thought—"

"But why," he asked, frowning again, "would you bring it *here*?"

Julie stared at him blankly. "Well, because she lives here!" But Carla's father kept looking at her with the same baffled expression. Julie faltered, "I mean, she *does* live here—doesn't she?"

The man shook his head. "No, I'm sorry. Carla lives quite a ways from here."

"Oh!" Julie felt embarrassed. Carla had definitely *never* mentioned that her parents were divorced. "She lives with her mother, you mean?"

The man set down his briefcase and took off his black coat. "Yes, of course," he said, hanging the coat on a coatrack in the corner. "Since her father isn't around anymore."

"B-but . . ." Julie stammered. It didn't make sense. "Aren't *you* her father? Aren't you Doctor — I mean *Detective*—Warner?"

The man gave a short laugh. "Not at all. I'm plain Mr. Anderson. And Carla's our—my—dog walker. She just comes here to walk Jack three times a week when I have to get home late from work, and sometimes on Sundays as well." He sighed. "I'm going to have to make some new arrangement, I'm afraid, now that my work schedule is changing again."

Jack nosed his way past the man and wriggled against Julie. She reached out absently and patted his head. What on earth was going on here? She felt as if the whole world had turned upside down.

"He likes you," the man said, glancing down

at the dog. "Jack doesn't usually take so quickly to strangers."

But I'm not a stranger. Julie narrowed her eyes in thought. *He met me yesterday, with Ivy. We played with him. He did tricks for us. Carla said he was her dog!* She bit her lip to keep from saying this to the man who was not Carla's father.

"Jack was my wife's dog," the man was saying quietly. "She always walked him in the afternoons. But Jane died a few months ago, and it's been hard for me to give the dog the amount of exercise he's used to. I was glad to hire Carla. She's been very good about coming here on the days I can't get home in time to walk Jack."

Julie tried to make sense of what he was saying. "Where *does* Carla live, then?" she asked the man abruptly. "Do you know?"

"On Appleby Street. Just a minute and I'll get the address for you." He disappeared into the kitchen, the dog following him. Julie waited in the front hall. Through the wide doorway into the living room she could see the framed photo of the gray-haired woman holding Jack when he was a puppy. The woman Carla had said was her grandmother.

What in the world was going on? Nothing made any sense.

The man returned with a slip of paper. He handed it to Julie. "It's a good walk from here. About nine or ten blocks."

"Thanks," she replied. Then she pointed to the photo. "Who is that with Jack in the picture?"

"That's my Jane." The man's voice was sad. "My wife. The house feels so big and empty without her. Jack and I are rattling around in it, aren't we, boy?" He patted the dog's head. "I'm gone so much of the time these days. What we really need is a housekeeper, not just a dog sitter, eh, boy? Breathe some life back into this place."

"Your wife looks . . . nice," said Julie awkwardly. "And Jack is so cute. I wish I could have a dog just like him! Well, um . . . good-bye."

She set off down the steps. She heard his voice call to her, "Hold on, wait just a minute. Why did you think Carla *lived* here?"

She hesitated, then turned. "I must have misunderstood her!" she called back. "Sorry about that!"

But I didn't *misunderstand*, Julie told herself as she walked down the steep hill. *Why did I think Carla lived there? Because—stupid me!—she told* me she did!

Her footsteps echoing sharply on the pavement, Julie walked as fast as she could in the growing dusk. She had to be home by dark, but she still needed to find Carla. She peered at the hastily scribbled address on the slip of paper in her hand.

All the little secrets, all the odd mysteries about Carla tumbled around in Julie's head as she walked, almost marching, along the streets, block after block, toward Appleby Street. But out of the jumble of mysteries, one harsh fact seemed unavoidable: Carla had lied.

She had said that she lived in the big green house, but Mr. Anderson said she didn't live there at all. She had said that Jack was her dog, but really he was Mr. Anderson's dog. She'd said

Mr. Anderson was her *father*, for goodness' sake, but he claimed that he was not.

As she walked, Julie tried to sort it all out—all the odd moments, the strange inconsistencies. Things Carla had said. Things Carla had not said. They were all pieces to the puzzle, which, if she could arrange them to form a whole picture, would solve the mystery of Carla Warner. Why should a girl who had so much—so many of the things Julie wished for herself—lie about her house, her dog, her dad, and her sister?

Julie stopped. She stood like a statue in the dusk. *A sister who wasn't a sister at all. And those brothers that nobody ever saw, who went to a school that nobody ever heard of . . .* Suddenly Julie *knew*. She still didn't know *why* Carla had lied, but Julie saw the web of lies woven bigger—and tighter—than she'd ever imagined. She felt betrayed.

When Julie started walking again, she moved faster, her anger propelling her along. *How dare she?* Julie thought furiously. Her face flushed with embarrassment at having been made such a fool of. *I thought she was my friend!*

She was so wrapped in her anger and humiliation that she barely noticed the car driving slowly alongside her. She looked up when the driver tapped the horn.

"Hey, babe," said Tracy with a wide grin. "Goin' my way?"

"Actually, not yet," said Julie. "I need to go to Appleby Street."

"That's a million miles from here! Well, at least five more blocks. What's on Appleby?"

"Carla," Julie snapped.

"Is something wrong?"

Julie shrugged. "I need to talk to her."

Tracy motioned Julie over to the station wagon. "Come on, get in. I'll be your taxi driver."

Even through her haze of anger, Julie had to smile at her sister's bright tone. Just put Tracy at the wheel of a car, and all was right in her world. *If only it could be as easy for me,* Julie thought. But all was definitely not right in Julie's world just now.

"Mom sent me to the store," Tracy was

explaining cheerfully. "I got *pounds* of fresh cranberries. Anyway, hop in! What's Carla's address?"

Julie opened the door and slid gratefully onto the vinyl seat. She dropped her heavy backpack onto the floor and consulted the slip of paper. "1867-C Appleby."

"Your wish is my command," Tracy said grandly as she pressed her foot down on the accelerator. The car shot up the street, block after block. Then she turned a corner and slowed.

"Eighteen-sixty-seven—there it is." Julie checked the address on the slip of paper as Tracy pulled up to the curb. The dilapidated apartment building was a far cry from the gracious Victorian house that Carla had bragged about. "I'll be back in a few minutes."

"Do you want me to park and come with you?"

"Can you just wait for me here?" Julie asked. She opened her backpack and withdrew Carla's homework. "I won't be long, believe me." It would take only a few seconds to tell Carla what she thought of all her lies. Julie got out of the car.

"No sweat," said Tracy, switching on the radio. "Born to Run," Tracy's favorite song by Bruce Springsteen, blared out. Tracy turned it up loud and started singing along.

Born to run, yeah, thought Julie as she approached the rundown apartment complex. *I've been running after Carla all afternoon. All week, really.*

Apartment C was around the back, on the third floor, at the top of a rickety wooden staircase. Julie climbed the steps determinedly. At the top was a narrow walkway with a wooden railing. Below Julie could see the parking lot, dumpsters overflowing with garbage. She walked along the outside corridor to Apartment C.

C for Carla, she thought. And then: *C for creepy*.

Julie rapped on the door, feeling each of the hollow thumps echo through the thin wood. She knocked again, but nobody came.

She turned and leaned out over the railing to look down into the parking lot, and across the street, for any sign of Carla. She could see Tracy waiting in the station wagon, but no Carla. She moved back to the apartment door and knocked again, harder than before. This time she heard a soft shuffle. Julie pounded until the door was finally opened.

Carla's dark hair was scraped back into an untidy ponytail. Her face was ashen. "What are you doing here?" she whispered. "I'm working on the case . . . You should . . ."

"I went to your house after school to bring you your homework," Julie interrupted brusquely. "Your house? That's a laugh. And that man—he's not your dad! He said you're his *dog walker*! Jack's not even your dog! The man gave me this address—he said you live *here*. Carla, what's going on?"

Carla stared at her with panicked eyes. *"Nothing."*

"But—then why—why are you lying to me?"

"No—I *didn't* lie. Well, okay, I did, about the house. But—"

Julie peered past her into the dim apartment.

"So this is your place?" Without waiting for permission, she pushed inside.

"Wait!" Carla blocked her progress. "Um—okay, yes, I do live here. I—I was just . . . *pretending* about the other house. We . . . we used to have a big house, and I miss it, so when I walk Jack, I like to imagine—"

Julie knew all about missing a big house. "I used to live in a big house, too. But I don't go around *lying* to people." Julie craned her neck to see past Carla.

There was just a small living room with a card table, two chairs, and a battered couch. The kitchen had enough room for only one person to stand in it at a time. The minuscule hallway led to a bathroom and two closed doors. The place was even tinier than Julie's own apartment above Gladrags.

Julie looked around. She saw no baby equipment. No children's toys—except a single doll, lying next to Carla's math book on the card table. Just two dishes in the dish rack, visible on the counter in the kitchen, and two mugs.

"Okay, so where are all your brothers and sisters?" Julie spoke in measured tones. "Where are they, Carla?"

"I'm here alone," Carla replied tonelessly. "Look—you'd better go."

But Julie stood there, eyes narrowed, her suspicions growing into certainty. She knew she was right about Carla's lies. But being right still left a hollow feeling inside her.

Carla reached out and shut the apartment door. She turned the lock until it clicked.

"So, where do all of you sleep?" demanded Julie, striding through the living room into the little hallway. "Where are the bedrooms?" She headed toward the two closed doors.

"No!" objected Carla. "Don't go in there. The—the baby is sleeping!"

"You said you were alone." Julie reached out and turned the knob of the first closed door. She pushed the door open to reveal a cramped bedroom with two single beds, unmade. There was a single dresser and a laundry basket with folded clothing stacked inside.

No baby, sleeping or awake.

"That's—my room," whispered Carla. "I share with—with Nancy. The baby sleeps in a crib in my parents' room. The other bedrooms are . . . through that door." Carla pointed to the closed door. "It leads to a hallway, with rooms on each side. Three more bedrooms for my brothers and parents—"

Carla put out her hands to stop her, but Julie strode forward and put her hand on the doorknob of the closed bedroom door.

"You can't just go in there!" Carla protested. But Julie twisted the knob and threw open the door.

There was no hallway at all. No three further bedrooms. Just a tiny linen closet, with a few sheets and threadbare towels folded on the shelves.

Hand on hips, Julie faced Carla. Her voice was low and quavering. "I figured it out."

Carla took a step back, as if wanting to run. Her lips trembled.

Julie stepped toward her. "There are no other bedrooms. There is no baby's crib." Another step, and Julie's voice grew louder and louder. She was shouting now. "There's no baby sleeping here. There isn't a baby, period. There's no kindergarten sister. No twin brother. *Nobody!* In fact, Carla Warner, you don't really have any brothers or sisters at all!"

11
SECOND CHANCES

"No! It isn't true!" whispered Carla. "I do! I have . . . I do have a brother. And I can explain about everything. It isn't what you think. The ogre—"

Julie waited.

"She—I was—I was *forced* to lie!" cried Carla. "She made me! She knew we were on her trail, about to make an arrest. Yes, she—"

Before Carla could finish, the outside door opened and a woman stepped inside the apartment. Her pinched frown looked fierce. Julie caught her breath. The ogre had a key!

Julie froze. This woman had threatened Carla with a knife and was now coming after her. Even the locked door had not kept her out. Quickly, Julie calculated their chances. If the ogre stepped any farther into the room, the girls could make a run for the door. Tracy was still in the car outside; she could drive them to the police station . . . Julie eyed the ogre warily, scanning for knives. But the woman, juggling two bags of groceries, had no hand free to wield a knife.

Julie blinked. *Groceries?*

The woman walked into the kitchen and set the bags on the counter. She turned, still frowning. "Why isn't the oven on?" she asked.

Julie gaped at her. Was this woman crazy as well as criminal? Then she looked past the ogre and saw, at the end of the kitchen counter, something shockingly familiar: the purple plastic lamp with the cracked shade and bright flowers.

"I asked you to have the casserole ready by five, Car. We need to eat early tonight, and I'm beat." Then the woman acknowledged Julie with a nod. "Hello there," she said. And to Carla she added, "Who's your friend?"

Carla flushed. "This is Julie. Um, Julie—this is . . ." She stopped.

Julie stared at the woman and, beyond her,

the lamp on the counter. Another puzzle piece slipped into place. "Your mom," she finished quietly. "Right? Barb is *your mom?*"

Shamefaced, Carla nodded.

The gaunt woman pushed her hair out of her eyes. "Please put the groceries away while I have a shower," she said. "We can heat up a can of soup. I've got to get to class by six." She looked over her shoulder at Julie. "It won't be much, but you're welcome to join us."

Julie shook her head. She felt dazed, her thoughts whirling. "No thanks . . . I've got to get home . . ." She had been angry before, but now she felt so overwhelmed, she could barely trust herself to speak.

Carla's mom shrugged, smiled wearily, and left the room. Julie just stood there, frozen.

Carla busied herself unpacking the bags while Julie watched. Apples, pears, broccoli, green beans, all slightly aged or spotted or bruised. "She gets to take stuff home from work at the end of the day," Carla mumbled. "For free."

"From Earthlight?" Julie inquired sharply. "Which is owned by Mr. Anderson?"

"Uh-huh." Carla glanced quickly at Julie, then away again.

"And she isn't a criminal, *actually*, is she?" Julie demanded. "Not a desperate villain that you and your detective dad are investigating. She might take useful things out of people's trash, but she isn't someone who would steal or do anything to hurt you—is she?" It wasn't really a question.

"No," whispered Carla. And now tears dropped soundlessly from under her lashes onto the groceries. "She's just my mom."

Julie's head was aching. She felt furious—and near tears herself. "What's *wrong* with you?" She fairly spat out the words.

"*Everything* is wrong with me," Carla sobbed, sinking down into a chair at the rickety card table. "My whole life is wrong."

Julie bit back her sympathy. Carla was crying brokenly and yet—and this was a scary thought—maybe even her tears were just an act.

Julie didn't move. Carla Warner was just a big huge jerk.

Hank's words echoed in Julie's head: *They don't mean to act like jerks; they just don't have the right words to tell how bad they're feeling.*

"Okay, tell me about it," Julie sighed, pulling out a chair at the card table. "Tell me everything. But this time—I want the *truth*."

"We used to live in Truckee, up in the mountains," Carla began softly. "My dad drove a snowplow and repaired ski lifts for the resorts—he's not a doctor or a detective, really—but then last year my parents divorced, and my dad moved out—all the way across the country to Vermont." Carla bit her lip. "He just *went*. We haven't seen him in a year, and he doesn't answer my letters," she murmured. "And he's behind—way behind—in the money he's supposed to pay Mom for child support. I don't think he even cares about us—about me—anymore." Carla's voice was swallowed by sobbing.

"But your mom cares about you, right?" Julie asked. "So why would you tell me she's a thief and an ogre? Why are you so mad at *her*?"

Carla gulped back her sobs. "I'm not mad at her—well, yeah, I guess maybe I am, sort of. It was bad enough having my dad move out, but *she's* the one who made us pack up and leave Truckee and my school and my friends and *everything!*"

Carla told Julie how her mom (not a doctor, not an ogre, but a housewife) had moved to San Francisco to find a job and go to college. One of her professors had a brother who owned Earthlight Farm, and the brother—Mr. Anderson— gave Carla's mom a job at the farmers' market. Carla described the long hours her mother worked to pay their living expenses and the college tuition. "She likes Earthlight," said Carla raggedly, "but it isn't great pay. Mr. Anderson lets me work there, too, on the weekends. And he hired me to walk his dog so that I could earn more money. We're saving up everything we can in order to rent a bigger apartment, with wheel-chair access."

"Why wheelchair access?" asked Julie.

Carla wiped her tears away with impatient fingers. "For Todd, my older brother."

"Oh, right—the one in college?" Julie shook her head. "No more lies, Carla."

Carla looked up at Julie. "It's not a lie. Todd is my *real* brother. He's twenty-two. If he hadn't gone off to Vietnam, he'd be in college now. He never wanted to go into the army. But he got drafted—and came home three years ago with both legs shattered. The doctors say he might never walk again."

Todd was a gifted musician and dreamed of being in a rock band, Carla explained. "It wasn't *all* a lie, the things I told you," she said beseechingly to Julie. "He *did* say I could be a singer in his band someday! But since he's been home from Vietnam, he's been in and out of the hospital having operations, and he won't play the saxophone anymore. My dad called him shell-shocked. Mom says that's a kind of trauma—when terrible things have happened to you and you just sort of shut down. When I go to see him, I can't bear it. He just sits and stares."

For a few months in the summer, Carla added, Todd tried living in a rehab place near their dad in Vermont. "But Dad never had any time for him." Carla's voice was taut, unhappy. "Todd seemed to be getting worse instead of better, so when Mom and I came to San Francisco, he came too, and moved into the rehab center here. We don't have a lot of time to see him, either, between work and school, but at least one of us visits him whenever we can, which is more than my dad did." She pressed her lips together.

"So that's where you were going when I saw you heading toward Market Street after school," Julie said tightly.

Carla nodded. "I couldn't let you know," she mumbled. "Not after I'd told you stupid lies about having other brothers. Healthy ones. Ones who played sports." Carla slumped at the table. "We're so worried about Todd," she whispered.

"He's just shut up inside himself, and he hardly even seems to care if we visit. He barely says a word when we're there. We won't even be seeing him on Thursday, because he's told us not to come. He says Thanksgiving is for suckers."

"I still don't get it," pressed Julie. "Of course it's terrible that Todd was hurt in the war, and it's sad that he's so depressed, but why so many *lies?*" There were things about her own life that she didn't like, but she couldn't imagine inventing a whole other life for herself. Why had Carla done it?

Tears streamed down Carla's cheeks again. "I just don't know, Julie! I've just been so sad and so *angry* about everything. I used to think we had the perfect family. And now ..." She wiped the tears with her fingers. "And then I had to start school and meet all those new kids who have normal lives and families ..." She swallowed hard. "I didn't know what to do," she whispered. "I just wanted everyone to like me."

"So you decided to make up a whole new family?" Julie's tone was brittle.

"I didn't really decide," Carla faltered. "It just sort of happened. It was sort of like writing a story—inventing the kind of family I wanted, rather than ..."

Her voice trailed off, but Julie finished the thought. "Rather than the one you have."

Carla nodded, shamefaced. "I know it's no excuse. I feel awful. Like—like somehow I killed off my whole family. But that's the thing with lies. Once you tell them—once they're out there—you're all tangled up in them. And they *stick*."

"And you're *stuck*."

"Oh, Julie, believe me—I have felt *so* stuck. I couldn't even go to school today, my stomach is in such knots." She rubbed away her tears and finally looked Julie in the eye. "My mom says I'm a good storyteller and that I should be a writer when I grow up. But she says sometimes my stories get away from me. And I think—I think she's right, because this time the stories turned into lies ... and one lie led to another." Tears welled in her eyes again. "It's no excuse."

"No, it really isn't," said Julie. She felt sorry for Carla, but still angry and, somehow, humiliated, too—as if by falling for Carla's lies, she had been the butt of a bad joke.

Carla blew her nose. "I'm s-sorry. I just wanted you to like me."

"I wanted to like you, too. I wanted to get to know you," Julie told her. "But I never knew the real you at all."

Carla looked away. "And now that you know what a liar I am, all the kids at school will know, and ... well, I don't blame you for not wanting to be friends. No one will want to be. No one will ever want to speak to me again." Her voice was very small.

Carla was right—and it was her own fault, Julie told herself. Who could trust her after so many lies? It was on the tip of her tongue to say so when the ogre—no, just Carla's mom—walked through the living room wearing a worn bathrobe, with a towel wrapped around her head.

She smiled tiredly at Julie. "Forgive me for not being a better hostess," she said. "It's so nice to meet one of Carla's new friends. I've heard about you! Your mom owns that cute shop, Gladrags, right? And your dad is a pilot?"

"Um—yes," Julie faltered.

"I'd love to own a shop someday," Barb said, reaching out to give her daughter a hug. "But first things first, as I always say—right, Car? First I need my degree so I can get a better job. And I couldn't do it without Carla. Do you know, she works two jobs after school and on weekends—helping at the farmers' market and dog walking—and gives me the money to help pay for food? I'll be glad when the day comes that she can keep her own money and spend it on herself."

Carla hugged her mom back.

Barb pointed to the bags of groceries. "I got us some extra goodies, honey," she said to Carla. "For Thanksgiving. It won't be much—and no turkey this year. But next year things will be better, you'll see."

"I don't want to have Thanksgiving if we can't even be with Todd," Carla muttered, tears spilling down her cheeks again. "There's nothing to be thankful for."

"But of course there is," said Barb, squeezing Carla's shoulders. "We have each other, don't we, babe? And I have *you*. What would I do without my girl?" She smiled at Julie again. "Carla gets up early on weekends to do errands for me. She goes to visit her brother every couple of days. And she does most of the cooking and cleaning, and has a cup of tea waiting for me when I get home late." She smoothed Carla's hair.

Barb's words touched Julie in a way that all of Carla's explanations had not. Carla's mom was talking about a girl that Julie didn't even know existed.

A girl who, maybe, deserved a second chance.

A peremptory rap on the door made them all jump. Barb opened the door. Tracy stood there, hands on hips. She peered curiously in at Julie. "Ready to go?"

Julie hastily shoved back her chair. "Oh, sorry.

We got . . . talking." She did not want to introduce Tracy to Barb, did not want to have to try explaining the whole complicated, crazy situation. She murmured a hasty good-bye and left with her sister. But then she turned to look back over her shoulder—and stopped.

Barb and Carla stood side by side in the doorway, both of them tall and thin, with their long dark hair swept back into ponytails—why had Julie not noticed the resemblance before?—Barb's arm still encircling Carla's narrow shoulders. They looked so much alike—and they reminded Julie of someone else she'd met recently.

Abruptly, Julie walked back to them. "Would you like to come for Thanksgiving dinner at our house?" Julie asked Barb. "Other guests are coming at three o'clock, and I know my mom would be happy if you came, too."

"Really?" Barb's eyes lit up. "How nice of you to invite us. Are you sure your parents won't mind?"

"There will be loads to eat," Tracy said. "Our

mom will call you tomorrow to confirm."

"See you on Thursday," said Julie. *You and your whole, huge family*, she thought bitterly to herself. Without looking at Carla, Julie left the apartment and followed Tracy to the car.

On the drive home, Julie sat silently in the front seat while Tracy sang along with the radio. As they were turning onto Redbud Street, Julie reached out and touched her sister's arm. "Wait, Trace. Can we stop at the rehab center? I need to—check on something. For Thanksgiving."

"We'd better make it fast," said Tracy. "Mom's going to worry if we're late for dinner."

Tracy waited at the curb while Julie ran inside the building and hurried to the reception desk. She took a deep breath and smiled at Ms. Joplin. "I've come to see Todd Warner," she announced.

Ms. Joplin looked surprised. "Well! You're the first visitor he's had, besides his family, I mean." She shook her head sorrowfully. "But I don't think he'll see you. Half the time he won't even see his mother and sister."

"Would you ask? Please?" Julie's anxiety mixed with determination made her voice sound shaky.

"All right. What was your name again, dear?"

"It's Julie Albright. But that won't mean anything to him." She paused, thinking. "Tell him that his brothers Tim and Tom sent me. And his sisters—Carla and Nancy and Baby Debbie."

Ms. Joplin jotted the names down on her scratch pad. She frowned. "I don't think—"

"*Please?*" pressed Julie.

The receptionist nodded. "All right. But don't get your hopes up." She left the room, and Julie stood with hands clenched until Ms. Joplin returned with an expression of surprise on her face. "I stand corrected," she told Julie. "He says to go in."

Julie entered the large room and saw the thin soldier in the wheelchair over by the windows, as before. She passed men who were reading and playing cards and watching TV. Some of them nodded and smiled at her. She crossed the room and stopped at the wheelchair. "Hello, Todd."

He looked up, his eyes dark pools in his thin face. "Who did you say sent you?" he demanded. "Tom and Tim and—who the heck?"

"Those are your brothers," Julie told him. "The ones Carla made up."

He frowned. "And who the heck are *you?*"

"I'm Julie. Carla and your mom are coming to our house for Thanksgiving, and Hank is bringing some of the other veterans. I want you to come, too."

"Thanksgiving?" He slapped his thin hands down on the blanket that covered his shattered legs. "Yeah—right. As if I have anything to be thankful for."

Julie took a deep breath. "Well, you have a sister who is really lonely and needs you in her life. Maybe you're not thankful for that, but it's true anyway."

"She doesn't need me. I'm no use to her." He glared at her.

"She invented a whole bunch of brothers and sisters because she's so lonely and sad without you," Julie stammered. "And I think it's *mean* that you won't even talk to her when she comes to visit!"

"It's none of your business," he said in a low voice. His sad, haunted eyes seemed to look right through her before he spun his wheelchair away.

Julie turned and left, feeling helpless.

At home Mom had dinner ready. "Where have you girls been?" she asked. "I was getting worried."

"It's my fault we're late," Julie said, and over dinner she told her mom and Tracy the story of Carla Warner—about all the lies, and as much of the truth as she knew. "So I hope you don't mind two more guests for Thanksgiving," Julie added.

"That deadbeat dad sounds like a rat," said Tracy.

"It's a hard situation," Mom said. "And it was wrong of Carla to make up all those lies. Still, I'm very proud of you for inviting Carla and her mother for Thanksgiving. That was a truly generous thing to do."

"Even if it's a squeeze," grumbled Tracy.

"How is everyone going to fit in this shoebox, that's what I want to know."

Mom ignored the grumbling. "It sounds like Mrs. Warner is doing the best she can. And with her college degree, she'll land a higher-paying job and be able to rent an apartment with wheelchair access for her son."

"I wonder if Hank knows him," Tracy said.

"Maybe he does," Mom replied. "We can ask Hank when he's here."

Julie drank her milk and didn't say a word. What was the point? Todd was clearly a hopeless case.

That night Julie lay in bed thinking about Carla—and about her own parents' divorce. She and Tracy didn't like it, yet Julie knew they were lucky that their parents were both very much a part of their lives. Unlike Carla's father, her dad *wanted* to see his children and be involved in their lives as much as possible. Julie even felt lucky to have Tracy. She wouldn't trade her sister—grumpy or not—for a whole pile of fake siblings.

Julie fell asleep watching Harriet the Spy-der, backlit against the window by the streetlight. Harriet's web had been damaged—perhaps by wind, perhaps by the rain. The spider was busy starting over again, weaving a new web.

12
THANKSGIVING

Thanksgiving morning was a flurry of preparations. As the apartment filled with the mouth-watering smell of roasting turkey, Julie and Tracy stood next to each other at the kitchen counter. Julie attached colorful paper feathers to the Pet Rock turkeys and fashioned little hats for the Pet Rock pilgrims, while Tracy peeled a mound of potatoes that would be boiled and mashed with butter and milk.

Julie finished the centerpiece scene by gluing little plastic googly eyes onto the rocks. "Look!" She held up a pilgrim for her sister to admire.

Tracy paused in her chopping and pointed her knife at Julie. "I'd better not find a stray eyeball staring up out of my mashed potatoes!" she warned teasingly.

As Julie watched her sister's sharp knife slice through the potatoes, she remembered how, at the farmers' market stall, Barb had pointed a knife at Carla. Now she knew Carla's mom had merely been gesturing while she spoke. Carla had never been in danger at all! Julie was glad about that, of course. But the real mystery now— the mystery of whether it was worth being friends with someone so untrustworthy—was harder to solve.

At two o'clock Hank arrived to set the wooden ramps over the steps leading from the sidewalk to the apartment. Then he poked his head into the kitchen, where the girls and Mrs. Albright were pouring pureed pumpkin into pie crusts. "I'm off to the rehab center now," he announced. "Tracy, will you come with me?"

Tracy looked at Mom. Julie knew her sister didn't want to go along but was too polite to say so.

"I need a driver," Hank told Tracy. "Someone to wait outside the center while I help the men into the van and load their wheelchairs."

If a *driver* was needed, that was a different story! Tracy ran to get her jacket.

Mom put the pies into the oven while Julie scurried around the apartment straightening up, plumping the pillows on the couch, and choosing records to play on the stereo for background music. Finally she surveyed the living room with approval. "Can I light some candles?"

Mom smiled. "Of course, honey. That will be the perfect final touch."

On the dot of three o'clock the doorbell pealed, and Julie ran to answer it. There stood Barb Warner, holding an Earthlight box full of apples and pears.

"Happy Thanksgiving!" she said to Julie and Mrs. Albright. "Thank you so much for inviting us!" She shook Mom's hand.

"It's lovely to meet you," Mom said, ushering Barb into the apartment. Carla sidled in behind her mother, an anxious expression on her face.

"Well, here we are," Carla said shyly to Julie as their mothers took the box of fruit into the kitchen. "Me and my one hundred siblings."

"I'll try to keep all the names straight," Julie quipped with a small smile.

Then they heard the front door open and the sound of laughter in the hallway. Mrs. Albright hurried to welcome everyone. Hank led the way into the apartment pushing one wheelchair, with Tracy right behind him pushing another. Behind them were two soldiers on crutches. Last of all came a third wheelchair—propelled by the thin, dark-eyed boy from the rehab center.

Carla gasped and turned to Julie with a stunned look on her face. Then she knelt down in front of the wheelchair and put her arms around her brother, resting her head against his chest. Watching them, Julie felt a sudden prick of tears behind her eyes.

Barb leaned over and hugged her son. "Oh, Todd," she said softly.

Todd hesitated and then put his arms around his mother and sister. Slowly he raised his head and met Julie's eyes.

Despite her astonishment that he had come, she kept her voice light. "Glad you could make it," she said, and felt a surge of satisfaction.

"Hello, hello, everyone! Please come in, all of you." Mom shook hands with all the veterans. The man called Tubby shyly presented her with a bouquet of lilies with his one good arm.

Hank came over to Julie. "Todd decided he wanted to come after all," he said quietly. "He told me that he'd been specially invited." Hank gave her shoulders a brief squeeze. "Thank you, Julie."

Everyone was shaking hands and introducing themselves, even Todd. When he came to Julie, he held out his hand formally. She took it.

His dark eyes studied her. "So—okay. I came." His voice sounded rusty.

"I'm glad," said Julie.

"I don't want a bunch of fake sisters and brothers taking my place," he said. "And I figure if my sister's friend comes all the way to the center to get on my case, I'd better show up."

Julie smiled weakly. But *was* she really Carla's friend? Could she be? *Carla deserves a second chance*, Julie reminded herself, but she still felt a heaviness inside.

As Todd turned his wheelchair away, Tracy leaned closer and whispered in Julie's ear, "He's so *dreamy!*"

Mrs. Albright invited everyone to come to the table. Everyone was crowded around together, but it worked, Julie thought happily, passing the mashed potatoes while Hank carved the turkey. All the guests seemed glad to be there. Even Todd glanced up from his plate from time to time at his mother and sister, and Julie saw his serious expression soften.

For a moment, as Julie looked around the table at them all, she saw—as if superimposed like a double-exposure photo—the faces of the family Carla had invented. The doctor/detective father next to Barb. The older college brother— that would be Todd. And then Tim, the high school brother, and Tom—Carla's twin. And then the kindergarten sister, Nancy, and of course baby Debbie. Their imagined faces wavered in the candlelight and then vanished.

Lies were powerful, Julie reflected. They took on their own sort of reality. That's why, when people told lies, it was hard ever to trust them again with the truth. She looked over at Carla, and then around the table at the faces of the other people—the people who were *really* there: James, Kenny, Abe, and Tubby. Todd and Barb and Hank. Tracy and Mom. She listened to their conversations. Tracy had been afraid the veterans would tell depressing war stories, but they didn't; instead they talked about their plans for the future. Kenny hoped to work in a bank. James and Abe had discussed setting up a travel agency together. Tubby wanted to go back to school and become an architect. "I used to build houses, back before I went to 'Nam," he told them. "But with just this one arm, I'm not sure how good I'd be on the construction end of things. Now I'd like to design the buildings myself. Make them accessible for disabled people, too."

Barb nodded. "Places that are wheelchair accessible are hard to find in this city. And hard to afford."

A vision of a house flashed in Julie's mind:

Carla's house that wasn't really Carla's house at all, of course, but would be perfect for her family—her actual family. A green painted lady *with an elevator*. Hadn't Mr. Anderson said he and Jack were just rattling around in all that space now that his wife had died? Hadn't he mentioned that he needed a housekeeper? A wonderful possibility formed in Julie's imagination. If only it could become real.

After the meal, Julie and Carla cleared the table and rinsed the dishes. Mom made coffee and tea while Hank and the other guests all moved into the living room. Julie and Carla stacked the plates in silence, feeling awkward. Suddenly Julie felt Carla's sharp elbow nudging her.

"Look!" Carla whispered. Julie turned. In a corner of the living room, Tracy sidled up to Todd with a stack of records and asked what sort of music he liked. There was a long moment of silence, and Julie thought he wasn't going to answer. But then he gave a fleeting smile and started telling her, in his raspy voice, about his favorites. Julie and Carla shared a knowing smile.

They wandered into Julie's bedroom. After all the laughter and chatter of the party, the room seemed extra quiet. Julie sat in her desk chair while Carla perched awkwardly on Julie's bed. At first Carla chattered about the weather—still foggy—and the holiday—mashed potatoes were her favorite food in the world—and then she turned to comment on photos that Julie had tacked to her bulletin board. "Ivy's so pretty," she chirped. "I love her hair. Oh, and who is that man in the uniform? A soldier?"

"That's my dad. He's a pilot."

"Oh—right."

The silence lengthened between the two girls, and they both looked out the window at the November dusk. Against the pane of glass they could see Harriet sitting in the middle of her new web.

"It is so . . . *wonderful*," said Carla, finally, "that you went to the rehab center and invited Todd specially. I don't know what you said to him, but it seemed to be the extra push he needed."

"I'm not the one who convinced him," said Julie. "Tom and Tim and Nancy and baby Debbie did."

At Carla's incredulous expression, Julie smiled. "Really! Ask him about it sometime."

Carla laughed shakily. "Okay, I will. I just can't believe he's in there now, talking about records with your sister."

The silence stretched between them again. Julie stared out the window. Then she looked at the girl sitting on her bed and took a deep breath. "Seems to me *you're* the one who has a whole lot of talking to do."

Carla met her eyes. "Oh, no. I think I've said enough already, don't you? More than enough?"

"No." Julie reached for her tape recorder, slipped in a cassette, and switched it on. "Hello San Francisco, this is KSPY radio. And now, the moment you have all been waiting for! Let me introduce to our studio audience the one and only, world-famous new girl in town—Carla Warner." Julie turned to Carla.

THANKSGIVING

"Now, then, Ms. Warner, please tell us about yourself. The people of San Francisco long to know the *real* you."

"Thank you, thank you," said Carla, taking the microphone. Her eyes crinkled up in the way that Julie liked so much. She tossed back her dark ponytail and smiled at Julie. "I am honored to be here with you today—and that's the absolutely unvarnished, plain and simple *truth*."

Julie glanced at the window, where the spider was wrapping up a fly with deft movements. Her own Thanksgiving feast in the new web.

The heavy gray fog outside seemed to be lifting. The heaviness inside Julie was lifting, too. Later, before Carla's family left today, Julie would tell them about her idea, about what Mr. Anderson had said. About how his house was too big for just him and his border collie. Maybe something could be worked out. Maybe Carla's story about living in that house wouldn't always be fiction.

Now Carla was also watching the spider intently. "Webs are incredibly sticky," she intoned into the microphone. Then she turned to Julie and spoke in her normal voice. "Very sticky—like lies."

"And like friends," Julie said, flashing a smile. "Friends *stick* together!"

> *O, what a tangled web we weave,*
> *When first we practice to deceive.*
> —*Sir Walter Scott*

LOOKING BACK

A PEEK INTO THE PAST

Steiner Street, San Francisco, in the 1970s

San Francisco is famous for its "painted ladies." There are many not far from Julie's neighborhood. These old Victorian houses are often painted in bright, cheerful colors rather than the pale hues found in most cities. They are admired for their elegant architecture and for their unique San Francisco character.

Today, many older buildings have been retro-fitted to permit wheelchair access, but when Julie was growing up, people were just becoming aware of this need. A woman named Judy Heumann, who used a wheelchair, and other activists urged the government to make public buildings accessible to people with disabilities. In 1973, Congress passed a law making it illegal to discriminate because of disabilities, but the law was never enforced. Four years later, in protest, Judy led a takeover of the federal government offices in San Francisco. For 26 days, hundreds of people sat in the offices, refusing to leave until the law's regulations were signed. Thanks to the actions of Judy and many others, the non-discrimination law was enforced, and public buildings have been made accessible to everyone—including people with disabilities.

Judy Heumann (in yellow socks) and disability rights activists

For disabled veterans like Todd, this new law would make it easier to attend college and get a job. However, like Todd, many Vietnam War veterans had other problems that couldn't be fixed just by passing a law.

These young soldiers typically entered the army at age 18 or 19, when they were still teenage boys. Some *enlisted*, or joined voluntarily; others were *drafted*, or ordered to join. In Vietnam, thousands of soldiers were killed or captured, and thousands more were badly injured. Even those who escaped physical injury were often

A soldier comes home to his family. He had been a POW, or prisoner of war, in a Vietnamese prison camp.

haunted by things they had seen and done during the war. Making matters worse, many soldiers didn't know why their country was at war or what they were fighting for. When they returned home, they found that millions of Americans did not support the war or believe the United States should be fighting in Vietnam at all. Because of the trauma of their wartime experiences, many Vietnam veterans became depressed or mentally ill, making it even harder for them to heal and get on with life.

As the war ended, thousands of Vietnamese orphans who were being adopted by American families were flown to the U.S. in the "Vietnam Babylift."

Veterans and people with disabilities were not the only Americans who believed that society needed to do a better job helping people live healthy lives. In the 1970s, Americans began focusing more on health and well-being in general. They started exercising more. They tried health practices such as yoga and meditation, which were new to this country. And they began paying closer attention to what they ate.

This popular book changed the way people thought about food.

Health-food stores first became popular in the 1970s.

Like Julie's dad, many people became aware that the typical American diet was too high in refined foods such as sugar and white flour. They learned that fresh, locally grown fruits and vegetables not only had more vitamins than canned ones but tasted better, too. Families started flocking to farmers' markets, where they could get freshly picked food from nearby farms.

Even restaurants got into the act. Across the San Francisco Bay in Berkeley, a young chef named Alice Waters opened a restaurant that served only fresh, local food, launching a trend that became known as California cuisine (quee-zeen). In the early 1970s, before farmers' markets were widely available, Alice sometimes had to get fresh fruits and vegetables from her neighbors' backyards and even vacant lots!

Alice also bought from local farms. To her daughter, Fanny, seeing the fresh harvest that arrived at the restaurant was like opening a present!

To meet the demand for fresh, seasonal, locally raised food, farmers' markets and health-food stores have become common throughout the country. What started as a seventies trend is recognized today as an important part of eating well and living a healthy lifestyle.

Today, girls enjoy helping at farmers' markets and vegetable stands.

ABOUT THE AUTHOR

Kathryn Reiss was a girl not much older than Julie in the 1970s. She grew up in Ohio but now lives in a Victorian-era house near San Francisco with her husband, five children, two cats, and a very clever border collie. She always loved reading mysteries and started writing them herself because nothing mysterious, eerie, or criminal ever seemed to be happening in her own neighborhood!

In fourth grade she told a whopper of a lie to a new girl at her school and quickly learned that honesty really is the best policy.

Kathryn Reiss's previous novels of suspense have won many awards. She teaches creative writing at Mills College. She loves to travel with her family and have afternoon tea in her garden with friends—and she is always hard at work on a new story.